Trial of Honor: A Novel of a Court-Martial

David Norton Stone

DEDICATION

To G.V., at last,

and, with the greatest respect, to the officers of the United States Navy who are graduates of Officer Candidate School

A note on time: The events depicted in this novel take place a few years after the Gulf War ended.

A note on the cover image: In Rhode Island, anchor = hope.

.

PROLOGUE: CRYING FLAMES

"Is there any ice left up there, Dr. Dinopoulis?" I asked.

"Getting thin. About twelve feet."

"So New York and Washington won't be under water any time soon?"
I loved to get him going.

"Not tomorrow. But I wouldn't invest in coastal real estate if I were
you," he answered.

The boat had five civilian scientists aboard. It was an idea which the
Great Lovers might have cooked up. The Navy was allowing
researchers onto its fleet of submarines to study the ocean. The Arctic
Ocean in particular. There the effects of global warming and ozone
depletion could be measured by studying change in the ice cover. That
was Dr. D's domain.

In the wardroom we called him Dr. Dread because of his dire predictions
about the melting ice cap. He constantly complained that the

experiments of the four other scientists took time away from his ice measurements.

"Will Dr. Small have the crew counting fish again this morning, Ensign Gunderson?"

"Yes, sir. You know that this mission is shared by five scientists. But just between you and me…?"

"Yes?"

"Your work is the most important."

"Of course it is."

In truth, Dr. Small's research interested me more. He collected data on fish populations and migrations. I couldn't decide whether his goal was to help the fish or fishermen. When I asked him, he answered, "Neither." He also collected information about the ocean floor in order to benefit…nobody.

As Supply Officer, I stocked and kept track of the equipment for the experiments, as well as for the whole boat. I was also in charge of the food service operation. After currying favor with Dr. Dinopoulis, I visited Dr. Small.

"Do you have everything you need, Dr. Big? Is the chow as good as the Columbia dining hall?"

"Can't tell the difference," he replied amiably.

"That bad! Sorry."

We were twenty-three days out on our thirty-five day cruise. In a few days we would give the scientists a treat by taking them beneath the North Pole, placing the diving planes in a vertical position so, as the seasoned sailors had me believe, we would burst through the ice above.

It would be a treat for me as well. I wanted to boast that I was the first Great Lover to stand at the North Pole.

It was a little after 0000, midnight. Day and night are of no consequence on a submarine. The three other scientists would begin their work again at noon, after Dr. D. and Dr. Small went to bed. Secure that my geniuses were content, I headed aft to the stores hatch from the control room. I was thinking about the pleasure of describing the Pole to my friends when someone behind me called my name.

"Ensign Gunderson?"

I recognized that voice. It was Commander Moeur, the executive officer. XO's do the dirty work of the skipper. I assumed something I had done or failed to had ticked off the Old Man.

I executed an about-face in the narrow passageway.

"Yes, sir?"

He walked toward me but didn't speak. I heard footsteps behind me and moved to the right to allow the men to pass. They didn't go by however. No, they held my arms while my XO informed me that the Captain requested my presence in his stateroom. I descended the ladder to the second level between the two guards.

The Captain, scratching his midnight beard, said, "Ensign Gunderson, I've been instructed by Commander SUBGRU 2 to place you under confinement until we return to Groton. A guard will be placed over you at all times. There is probably cause to believe than an offense under the Uniform Code of Military Justice has been committed by you. While we are at sea, you will not be interrogated, and you do not have to make a statement. Any statement you make, however, may be used against you. That ends the speech I've been told to make. On a more personal note, I qualified for my dolphins twenty-five years ago and, in

5

a quarter century as a bubblehead, I've never known this to happen on a submarine. I can't spare the room for your cell, and I can't spare the men for your guards. But I have no choice. Any monkey business and I'll fire you out the TDU."

The TDU was the Trash Disposal Unit, which ejects garbage cans like torpedoes are launched.

I decided it wasn't going to do any good to apologize.

*

The boat surfaced. First through water, then ice. These tin cans are made for floating though water, not sitting in it. We took roll after nauseating toll. The guard changed outside my door. "Get up there," I heard one say to the other. "It's the top of the world." Until the last minute I believed I would be allowed onto the bridge, to pose for a snapshot. The boat sank. I felt like a person who had climbed Mt. Everest and been blindfolded at the summit.

All because I was a Great Lover.... Our society existed to help the Navy, not harm it. It was a misunderstanding, one that James was probably clarifying at that very moment.

*

During the months I awaited court-martialing, I pieced together what occurred on the surface of the world while I floated with scientists under the Arctic Ocean. Two weeks before I was placed under confinement on the submarine, there was a disturbance in the scale-pans of international relations. The nation that maligned the balance of power was China.

This was the situation, one in which a Great Lover would play a role. The Chinese were conducting live missile firing exercises off the coast

6

of Taiwan. Not coincidentally, this show of might happened during an election in Taiwan. China hoped to annex Taiwan someday like it was taking over Hong Kong in 1997. But the front runner in the Taiwan presidential election was known to be anti-unification. By exploding missiles near two major Taiwanese ports, China sent a clear message.

To protect the integrity of the election and to prevent a possible Chinese invasion, President Clinton sent the aircraft carrier *Determination* and its battle group into international waters 200 miles southeast of Taiwan, just outside the zone closed by the Chinese for live fire testing.

James Drayton was one of the intelligence officers on the *Determination*.

*

The carrier is on low level alert, with armed planes ready to take off in sixty minutes notice. Ensign James Drayton has an uneventful watch until 0541, when a fast moving object appears on his screen, where the exclusion zone is marked by four green boxes with connecting lines. It is a Chinese M-9 ballistic missile. The missile explodes twenty miles from the port at Kaohsiung. James decides not to wake the commanding officer. He has instructions to do so immediately if China intentionally or accidentally destroys a Taiwanese or American target. This was just a water churner.

James's relief arrives at 0600. He passes down the information from the night watch and walks to the officer's wardroom for breakfast. The most recent missile firing is stale news there. CNN reported it only moments after the Navy's own satellite and radar systems detected it.

James eats pancakes and half a grapefruit and heads to his rack for a couple of hours of shuteye. He has an appointment at 1030.

*

When they transported him to the hospital ship, two of his friends remained at his side to show that this victim was different, special, loved. Through their shock, they attempted to communicate this information about James to his doctors and nurses. To the great relief of these friends, who were named Lt. Baronne and Lt. Brown, the people tending to James professed to understand this. They were actually quite adept at pretending to understand the uniqueness of their patients. It was useful in getting quivering lieutenants away from the injured.

"The other four died instantaneously," Brown and Baronne told anyone who would listen on the hospital ship.

One of the nurses said, "It's unbelievable that your friend is doing so well then. That explosion is going to have one survivor anyway."

Really, saying the right thing was an art form on the hospital ship. It was another form of healing.

Baronne and Brown returned to the aircraft carrier, confident their friend would recover, excited to deliver the good news to shipmates. Until they saw the ugly buckling, like an eyebrow, on the carrier deck. Beneath it, warped steel sang of hell.

The explosion was an embarrassment to the Navy and jeopardized the Taiwan Straits mission. The *Determination* limped back to Japan before another carrier could arrive on the scene. The Chinese laughed at this failed U.S. attempt at gunboat diplomacy.

This is what was immediately known. Four sailors were killed, one gravely injured, while arming weapons below decks for the fighter plans above. The cause of the explosion was a mystery. The names of the victims were withheld pending notification of the families.

The Captain of the ship, however, knew who was involved, and his surprise would later be echoed by many others.

WHAT THE HELL WAS AN OFFICER DOING DOWN THERE?

*

On April 23, 1915 he died on a French hospital ship off the Greek island of Skyros. They buried him on a hill in Skyros, in a grave marked by a simple white cross. Britain knew immediately what she had lost – her greatest poet, her kindest heart, her finest man, who gladly gave his most precious gift, his life, to her.

*

The *Determination* had never known an officer quite like Ensign Drayton. In addition to his intelligence work and his collateral duties, he helped and observed in every department of the ship. To the Great Lovers, who hoped one day to eliminate the officer/enlisted distinction, this was estimable behavior. No job was too dirty for him, no task too trivial. To his shipmates this was an accepted eccentricity...at least until the explosion.

How quickly sorrow turned to suspicion when the Navy demanded answers for the explosion. What was an officer doing down there? Who was James Leo Drayton? At first they wondered why he lived when others died. Then they noted that he simply died last, three days after the others, in an American hospital in Japan.

From the start, James had warned all of us not to express anything about the Great Lovers in writing. He himself was meticulous in this regard. I know this because when the Naval Criminal Investigative Service searched James's possessions they came up with nothing incriminating. Only when they combed through the furnishings of the Norfolk beach house (they sat in storage in Virginia) did they locate a key to our society's existence. In a box of books, they found an otherwise empty notebook that contained an unfinished letter, dated Memorial Day weekend a year earlier. Addressed to "Dear Tate", it said:

"I am still trying to understand why you kissed me last night. My attraction to you is something I have struggled to conceal, to deny to myself. Did I dream your kiss, because the one thing I know with certainty about you is that you are heterosexual!

What I hope…I hope you kissed me because, sensitive as you are, you understand my conflicted feelings and, generous as you are, you wanted to give me as much as you are able.

What I fear…Your kiss was a power play of some sort, like a male cat spraying to mark his territory. Do you resent or covet my hold on the others?

This is likely to be the last reunion of the Great Lovers for some time, and I don't want it to be spoiled. Another matter. For too long I have not contradicted your claim that you are the accidental member of the Great Lovers, that you were included only because fate made you my roommate. This is not true…" The letter abruptly ended there.

This forgotten, half-written letter told its finders that James was gay, hinted at a group called the Great Lovers, provided the makings of a motive for an explosion.

It was not difficult to identify "Tate." A Tate Gunderson was the beneficiary of James's Navy General Credit Union insurance policy. Nor was it difficult to discover who was at James's beach cottage that Memorial Day.

They had the Great Lovers.

They had me, Tate Gunderson.

PART ONE: HIGH SECRETS

"These I have loved...," James Drayton read in a whisper on the October night the Great Lovers Society was formed.

It was 2230, after "lights out," and he had taken precautions to ensure we weren't discovered out of our racks. Racks were beds. He had stuffed a towel in the space between the deck (floor) and the bottom of our hatch (door) to prevent the little light in the room from attracting the patrol.

I probably would never have been chosen as a Great Lover if it weren't for the accident of being assigned to share a room with James. The other three were chosen for qualities they possessed, I assumed. The five of us barely knew each other then. We had only arrived at Naval Officer Candidate School a week before the night the secret society formed.

James finished reciting the poem and Chavez said he didn't understand it. None of us did, although Rayna Washington, Jennifer Levy and I wouldn't admit it.

"It doesn't matter if you don't get it now," James assured us. "You will soon enough once you memorize it. The poem 'The Great Lover' is our Constitution, and the poet Rupert Brooke is our spiritual leader."

"I don't have time for your dead poet's society. What's the use of memorizing poetry at OCS? I thought this club of yours was supposed to help us all get through," Rayna complained.

"That's our first goal – commissions for all of us. And it won't be easy. I tapped you – Tate, Rayna, Jen, Chavez – because I think you need help. I also suspect you're the kind of officers the Navy needs."

"That's a good first goal. Help each other through OCS. But what's the point of the Great Lovers once we graduate?" I asked.

"To reform the Navy."

"Is this legal, to be forming a secret society? It seems so anti-authority."

"Listen to me, Jennifer. You're in the Navy, the service most dependent on team work and cooperation. Navy means ships. Ships require sailors to run them, working together in unison and cooperation. The best thing we can do right now to prepare for driving ships is to start working together as a team. Being a Great Lover is completely in synch with Navy philosophy."

"If teamwork is so important, why should just the five of us be involved? Hell, why not the whole battalion?" Chavez asked.

I could tell James didn't have an answer for his question. To support him I said, "It's just not possible. A big group is impractical."

James still looked troubled. He spoke.

"Someday the whole Navy will benefit from our ideas. I wish we could get everyone through OCS, but it's going to be hard enough with only you four hosers." Hosers was the OCS word for screw-ups, sailors who ought to be beaten with a hose.

"Speak for yourself," Rayna said.

But I knew James was right. Officer Candidate School was a hard road. Four months to learn what Academy midshipmen have four years to assimilate. In addition, none of us except Chavez had previous military experience.

James gave each of us a copy of the poem.

"To make it easier, just read it for now. Don't commit it to memory yet. Just try to understand. Tomorrow night we start getting each other through this challenge."

We turned off the light, opened the hatch and checked the hall.

"All's clear. See you next time. And don't forget. This is a SECRET society."

Chavez, Jennifer and Rayna returned to their rooms.

*

The wonder of it was not that an underground survival group formed at OCS, but that James Drayton should be the one to organize it. James was perfect and would excel without help from anyone else, I was sure.

The night after we first met, the Great Lovers convened again. James asked each of us to state what we believed to be our vulnerabilities.

One of us confessed to being a slow reader and a poor writer, another to having trouble with classes like piloting, celestial navigation and engineering.

"We'll get each other through. It's ridiculous that we have to learn some of these subjects. Ships sail themselves nowadays. It's just a throwback to Navy tradition."

"How are we going to get each other through, James? Are we going to get the gouge before the tests?"

By "the gouge," Rayna meant the answers.

"No way. The Great Lovers don't cheat. Under no circumstances will we find justification to cheat. If you know that anyone else is cheating you're bound by the honor code to turn him or her in. If any of you cheat, I'll turn you in. Tate, what do you need help with?"

"I can't shine shoes, make a bed, wear the uniform right. That kind of stuff."

"That's the easy part," Chavez said.

"Not for Tate," James said in my defense. "He's never had any discipline. You were an enlisted Marine, Chavez. You're squared away in all that stuff. You help us all with our shoes and belt buckles."

The only one who hadn't owned up to a weakness was Jennifer. James called her out on it.

"To be honest, I really don't think I'm going to have a problem. I'm glad to lend a hand to the rest of you though."

"PT, Jennifer," said James. "Physical Training. Are you going to pass? You're twenty pounds overweight."

"I am not."

No one rushed to Jennifer's defense.

"What did you have for chow tonight?" James asked her.

"I don't remember. Wait, yes I do. A salad."

"I watched you. You ate mashed potatoes, macaroni and cheese, corn and a little bit of salad drenched in blue cheese dressing. We're all going to get a fitness medal. The standards for push-ups and sit-ups are a joke, but as far as I can judge, the run is going to be a problem for all of you except Rayna. A mile and half in nine minutes. That's a six minute mile.'

"There's no way I can do that," Jennifer admitted.

"There is a way. Training. We'll start tomorrow."

"Your turn, James," I said.

"I'm not going to tell you where I need help yet. Somebody tell me what 'inenarrable' means. No one knows? It's in the poem. You were supposed to read it. Always, no matter what you're reading, if you don't know a word stop immediately and look it up. Read the poem again. Understand it before you memorize it."

Chavez mumbled something.

"Speak up, Chavez," James said.

"That word isn't in the dictionary. I looked it up last night."

"What? Let me see."

We all had the same Navy issue dictionary on our desks.

"Good man! At least you tried. Noah Webster is rolling over in his grave. I'll give you the meaning, since it's not in the dictionary. It means 'unable to be told, unspeakable.' This meeting of the Great Lovers has concluded."

*

Jennifer asked, "Where is Mataiea?"

At the end of the poem the place and date of its completions appeared: MATAIEA, 1914.

"It's in Tahiti," James answered solemnly.

"Was he fighting in Tahiti?"

"No...."

"Because this is the poem of a soldier prepared to die, saying goodbye to all the things he loved. Bread, blankets, flowers. Comfortable smelling fingers, whatever that's supposed to mean."

"It's a nice poem, James, but I've never heard of Rupert Brooke. You seem to know a lot about him. Was he a *****?" I asked.

James stood and walked to the window of the room we shared. He turned, came to where I sat and punched me hard on the arm.

"Take it easy. There aren't any gay people in the Navy," I joked, "so I couldn't have offended anyone."

He punched me again in the same spot.

"Leave him alone, James," Chavez ordered. "I wondered the same thing about this guy. It's the line about how he loved blankets."

"'The rough male kiss of blankets.' That's what you're talking about? Didn't you guys have fathers who kissed you goodnight? He's comparing the scratchiness of wool blankets to his dad's five o'clock shadow."

"Why did you get so mad at Tate?" Rayna questioned him. "You really idolize Rupert Brooke, don't you?"

"That's not why I punched Tate."

"Why DID you hit me then? Twice!"

"You insulted me."

"I insulted Rupert Brooke."

"You hurt me. Don't you understand?"

"What do you mean? You're not...?" I couldn't complete the sentence. "Are you?"

James was standing near the desk. The lamp illuminated his face from below. Although the lighting made James look tortured and ghostly, nothing could make his appearance terrible. That's what made it impossible that he could be....

The first thing I thought about James when I met him was that he could probably have any woman he wanted. I stood in line behind him the first day at OCS when we waited in our skivvies to be measured and weighed.

"James Leo Drayton," he told the corpsman confidently. The corpsman asked James a question, which he answered affirmatively. Then the Navy health specialist read aloud the measurements to his assistant.

"71 inches, 165 pounds."

Then the corpsman wished James good luck and signaled me forward. He didn't ask me anything other than my name and didn't offer me his best wishes. I thought it was because of the unimpressiveness of my measurements. 68 inches, 156 pounds.

James had dishwater hair and small blue eyes. He had thin lips often pursed into a disapproving expression. His chin was weak above such a long neck. But these imperfections weren't something I noticed right away. I only pinpointed them after something bigger had registered. James belonged to the nobility of men. He had a presence. He was commanding. He had class.

As I said, his features didn't really make the effect. It was something else, which I feared might be good breeding. Feared because that meant I could never hope to attain for myself what set him apart. I guess I hoped it was an acquired quality of intellect or spirituality that give him his presence rather than rich parents.

How could James, my hero, be an undesirable, officially invisible, one of those people the Navy deemed fit only for immediate discharge? I knew Chavez looked up to James like I did. I was sure both Rayna and Jennifer were in love with him.

"Did you think I wasn't going to need any help from you? I can pass the classes, I could get the fitness medal today. But I'm an infiltrator. I have to hide my identity to stay here, and that makes me furious. 'Don't ask, don't tell' sucks as a policy. You have to save me from my anger, from telling. Tate, I'm sorry I punched you. You all have to help me to not deck anyone else. I wanted all of you to know so I don't feel so isolated. Let's call it a night."

*

In addition to my initial amazement, I had another reaction to James's revelation: relief. He had an Achilles heel like the rest of us. He also would not be competing with me for Jennifer's affection.

At the next meeting of the Great Lovers Chavez spoke first.

"I want to talk about what you admitted last night, James."

"I expected that."

"I want us to discuss it with you out of the room."

"Is this a coup d'état?" Rayna joked.

"Listen. I'm Navy first and Great Lover second. As future Navy officers we have a duty that goes beyond friendship," Chavez reminded us.

"I'll come back in fifteen," James said.

As soon as he was gone, Jennifer laid into Chavez.

"His sexual orientation has nothing to do with whether he can fight in a war."

"The policy says, 'Don't ask, don't tell.' He told. We have to turn him in."

"Technically, you're right. We should. Who wants to go to the commanding officer?" Jennifer asked.

No one accepted the job.

"Why don't you do it, Tate. Don't you care that you have to sleep in the same room with him?"

"Jesus, Chavez. Maybe I shouldn't be in the same room with you now," Rayna said.

"You do it, Chavez," I told him.

He stood and walked to the door. It was over for James. Then Chavez swore and sat down on my bed again.

"He's a good guy. He could have just kept his mouth shut and got his commission without any help from us. He's squared away. It was pretty Navy of him to help four other people through with him. The day I got here I saw everyone else as competition. James showed me we're all shipmates. No, I'm not turning him in. The Navy is wrong about James."

When James came back, Chavez faced him eye to eye.

"James Drayton, the Great Lovers have decided. It's all for one and one for all, buddy. In fifteen weeks we're ALL going to be Ensigns."

Chavez hugged James. The weak link in the Great Lovers proved to be strong.

That's when the Great Lovers really began, the night we chose a friend over our country.

*

The night of our first liberty since arriving at OCS, the first time we were allowed to leave Coddington Point in two weeks, James suggested that the Great Lovers meet at a many starred French restaurant on a wharf in Newport.

James, Jennifer, Rayna and I couldn't wait to escape and signed out at 1801, the first possible moment. Our reservations weren't until 2000, and Chavez said he needed a nap and would meet us at the restaurant. It was heaven to walk aimlessly down a sidewalk again, to poke carelessly though CD bins, to savor a beer at a pub full of civilians and know that I was doing something for them, going places.

I craved pizza, but the place James chose had a major advantage. No other officer candidates would go to such a swanky place. We did not want anyone to know the Great Lovers existed, working hard to avoid each other's company during our days. Only after lights out did we meet in the privacy of James's and my room. Or, during liberty, at restaurants with twenty-five dollar entrees.

We ate nothing but bread for the first half hour. I wasn't really happy with the seating arrangements. It was a round table set for five. To my right was the seat reserved for Chavez. James sat to my left. James had Jennifer on his other side, and Rayna sat next to her.

We decided that Chavez wasn't going to awaken from his nap and ordered. Steak for me. Jennifer conferred with James and they had the same dish – bouillabaisse. Rayna wanted the half chicken.

"That smells delicious," I told James.

"Tastes even better," Jennifer answered.

"I'm surprised James lets you eat, Jennifer," I joked.

"I've lost five pounds. I'm entitled to a reward."

"Have a bite," James invited.

"I'm fine with just my steak."

"Come on, Tate. Try some." James put a delicate white clam on my plate.

"Give him a scallop too," Jennifer said. 'They're heavenly."

Before I knew it, James was holding his fork in front of my mouth. If the scallop were on the end of Jennifer's fork I know I would have accepted it. But I could not bring myself to let James feed me.

"I don't care for them, James. I'll try the clam though."

I could tell he felt insulted, and I wished I could take back my squeamish refusal. Since I couldn't without looking weird, I patted his leg instead. He was saying something to Jennifer at the time and his head jerked suddenly towards me. The only thanks I got for my apology was a creased forehead.

We were back at the base by 2300. I checked the log to see if Chavez had ever signed out.

"Hey guys. Chavez signed out not long after us, and he still isn't back."

"Maybe he couldn't find the restaurant," Rayna said.

*

The next morning Chavez had a black eye and several small cuts on his face. We didn't hear the story until the Great Lovers met that night.

His lower lip was swollen, forcing Chavez to speak with more delicacy than usual.

"I went to a bar I heard about," he said.

"Do you have a drinking problem?" Rayna asked.

"I have a problem, but it's not drinking. I'm not cut out to be an officer. I hated just about every officer I met in the Marines. Now I'm surrounded by those types twenty-four hours a day. You wanted me to meet you at a French restaurant. Instead I went to a place where you wouldn't be caught dead. Sitting on a barstool there was the first time I felt like myself in a while."

"Home sweet home," Jennifer said. "Who who beat you up?"

"I did the beating. The guy next to me could tell I was Navy by my gorgeous haircut."

"He could tell from your uniform too," James said.

"I wasn't wearing it."

"You know we're not allowed to wear civilian clothes."

"I wasn't feeling very law abiding last night. Maybe I had too much to drink. The guy just looked at me funny and I threw him onto the pool table."

"You kicked a townie's ass and then took on the whole bar? Very courageous," Rayna commented.

"Are you kidding? I ran out of there as fast as I could."

"What happened to your face then?"

"I bumped into a couple of fists at the exit."

"If you go to those kinds of places, you're going to find a fight," I warned him.

"That's why I went to that place, Tate. I was hungry for a brawl."

"I take full responsibility for this," James said. 'I should have foreseen it."

"How could you predict it, James. You don't even really know me."

"That's what I'm talking about. I've been worrying too much about the curriculum and not enough about personality."

"It's not your fault, man. If Chavez had gone out with the rest of us this never would have happened. Have you ever heard of conduct unbecoming an officer? You epitomized it last night. If the police were called to that bar you'd be out of OCS."

"Easy Tate," James said. "Let me tell you what worries me. Chavez feels alienated from the others here, different, a traitor to his old self. Let me ask you something, Chavez. How did you get from being an enlisted Marine to here? You had to work for a bachelor's degree first. How long did that take you?"

"Seven years of night classes."

"Why did you put yourself through that?"

"To come here," Chavez admitted.

"So there used to be two of you, right? One was the regular guy Marine during the day. He had a chip on his shoulder. The other was the striker at night school, a man with an eye on the future, someone a little more ambitious than his buddies. You have to choose which of these personalities is really you, Chavez. Who do you want to be? I think the fact that you made it all the way to OCS answers that question."

"Striker" is slang for an ambitious sailor.

"I don't want to be the angry one. Not the cynical, complaining grunt." He put his face in his hands. Carefully.

"You're not, Chavez. That's not you," James assured him.

*

After the meeting that night, when the others had returned to their rooms, James asked me who I was.

"What do you mean?"

"I realized tonight I didn't know Chavez. Now I wonder about you, Jennifer, Rayna."

"James, we're never going to know each other's minds completely. I think Chavez was as surprised as the rest of us about what happened to him last night."

"Autobiographies. That's what we need."

"Come on. We're busy enough. As it is, we spend half our meetings on things other than class work."

"It won't take long to hear five more. Chavez already gave us his."

"But there are only four more then. Unless you invited someone else."

"Rupert Brooke is the other Great Lover, Tate. Never forget him."

*

At the next meeting of the Great Lovers, Jennifer was telling us her history, when I heard the door open, and a voice not belonging to any Great Lover asked, "What's going on?"

I recognized the chubby face as it drew closer to the dim light on the desk. Chavez was poised to attack. I whispered to him to relax.

"Ryan, do you know how to knock?" James asked. "Chavez almost ripped your throat out."

Ryan Morrissey had the room next to me and James all to himself. There was an odd number of men in our Company and Ryan lucked into a single room. Knowing what I gained from living with James I no longer envied Ryan his private suite.

"For two weeks I've been hearing you talk in here after lights out. Who else is here? Miss Levy…Miss Washington. Boys and girls, what ARE you doing?"

"It's just a study group," Jennifer lied.

"Can I join?"

"No, Ryan. Start your own," James said.

"Sorry to mention it but, um, where are the books?"

"You caught us. We're plotting a mutiny. We surrender. You'll probably get the Congressional Medal of Honor. Now, please get out of my room."

"You don't know how much I've heard. You better not talk to me like that, Drayton. I don't care that you father was CNO."

CNO. Chief of Naval Operation. In the eighties that post had been held by Michael Drayton. Was he James's father? I could tell the other Great Lovers were as surprised as I to hear this. Then again, we hadn't yet heard James's autobiography. Still, this was something he should have mentioned by now. That explained the extra attention he'd been getting from some of the regular Navy people at OCS, like the medic at weigh-in who wished him luck.

"Tate, please show this garbage out of our room."

I pushed Ryan into the hall and shut the door.

"Thank you, Ambele," James said.

"What did you call me?"

"Never mind. Obviously, we can't meet here anymore. I'll tell you plan B tomorrow."

*

"Are you still awake, James?"

"Yes, Ambele."

"What the hell does that name mean?"

"In time I'll tell you."

I hoped Ambele was "friend" in James's private language.

*

James judged it unsafe for us to meet as a group at OCS any longer. Ryan would eavesdrop on any meetings held in the room James and I shared, and the walls of the other Great Lovers had ears as well. But were we really guilty of anything worse than ignoring "Lights out?"

I asked James that question one afternoon at lunch, when he and I ate together at one table, Rayna and Chavez sat together at another and Jennifer dined somewhere else with Ryan of all people.

"I'm worried about a few things," James said. "One is a cheating scandal. All five of us meeting together and, coincidentally, getting the top grades. That looks bad."

"But the Great Lovers are opposed to cheating! It's in our charter."

"I know that. But people might think we're a gouge club."

"We're tops in everything, even in PT and military bearing, which are impossible to cheat at."

"I'm afraid of another accusation. Treason."

I laughed. "What's treasonous about Jennifer telling us her history or my own inspirational life story."

"You don't think very much of yourself. It's one of your best qualities."

"Where do you come up with treason?"

"We haven't arrived at that aspect of the Great Lovers in our meetings yet. But I have to admit that some of my ideas are radical. Not a danger to the country, but to the structure of the military. I'm going to introduce what I believe in at the next sessions. Don't worry. You'll find that I'm motivated by patriotism. Wait until Saturday before you make any judgments."

"Where are we getting together anyway?"

"Boston. Birthplace of Freedom."

James stared at Ryan for the rest of the meal. Somehow, I didn't think he was going to graduate.

*

"I love the city!" Chavez yelled.

The Great Lovers obstructed the passing of other pedestrians on the sidewalk in front of South Station. Other officer candidates had taken the bus to Boston with us, including Ryan Morrissey. They were all sightseeing together; the *USS Constitution*, Old North Church and the *Cheers* bar. Ryan looked back at us as he departed with that group.

"So much for a secret meeting," Rayna complained.

James smiled at Jennifer. I didn't understand why, but Jennifer and Ryan were spending a lot of time together. Was the overweight meddler no longer a threat?

"I want to see the *Constitution* too," I whined.

"Not today," James stated. "We're on a pilgrimage."

"I'm not going to any churches," Chavez said.

"Not a religious pilgrimage, at least not in the way you're thinking. You know that poem you all memorized. Today we're going to visit a few of the places that were important to its author, Rupert Brooke."

"He was English," I said.

"Yes, but he travelled to America twice."

James walked jauntily to the Red Line entrance of the subway. The rest of us followed unenthusiastically.

"I'd rather walk the Freedom Trail," Chavez muttered.

James exited the subway at Charles Street, and the rest of us raced out behind him before the door closed.

"That's Beacon Hill on the left," Jennifer said.

"You went to college here, didn't you?" I asked.

She nodded. "Civilization is even better than I remembered. Stop, James!" She yelled. "This bakery has the best strawberry muffins in the world. I've lost seven pounds and I'm having one."

James agreed. "We have to feed the body and the soul."

The café was on the first floor of a deconsecrated church. Jennifer and James had strawberry muffins. Rayna and Chavez ordered calzones. The guy behind the counter stared at me as I looked for something I couldn't get at OCS. It suddenly struck me that to the man behind the counter I must look like the odd man out. Jennifer-James and Rayna-Chavez could be two couples, I thought, looking to the table where they sat eating.

When I finally sat down, Rayna whispered, "Don't be jealous."

I was too surprised to say anything then, but I made sure Rayna and I fell behind the others when we resumed walking.

"I'm sorry if I embarrassed you, Tate, but the fact that you're in lust with Jennifer is obvious. You know that she and James are never going to amount to anything. Great friends maybe, but not great lovers. She's infatuated with him right now. Look at the swans."

We were in the Public Garden. Swans in pairs maneuvered around the kidney shaped lagoon. The water looked grayer than the sky. I thought they must be cold. My pea coat kept me so warm it had deceived me into thinking it was a nice day.

I had to respond to Rayna.

"Please don't say anything to Jennifer about what you've noticed. You're wrong about one thing, though. It's love, not lust."

Rayna just laughed, and I did too, vowing to stop taking myself so seriously.

The other three were waiting at the corner for us.

"You can see it from here," James said, pointing to a brownstone. Even when we stood at the bottom of its steps, I couldn't see anything special about it.

"This is the office of the *Atlantic Monthly*. On his way to the South Seas, Rupert visited several cities in the United States and Canada. The year was 1913, and he was twenty-five years old. At that age, he had published one volume of poetry and contributed to a best-selling collection, *The New Georgians*. He wasn't a household name – yet – but literary people knew of him here and he met some of them on his way across the continent.

"He stood here, double-checked the address and then climbed these stairs. Now I'm going to tell you one of the most important things about Rupert. He had beauty of face. At least, that's how people always put it back then." His listeners chuckled and James blushed.

"Not beauty of body, like me?" Rayna asked.

"His body was ideal too, I think, for that time. He was almost six feet, 165 pounds. A little thin by today's standards."

I had stood behind James the day we were all measured and weighed. Those were his statistics too.

"Rupert was a gentleman, educated at a British public school. That's what the English call their boarding schools."

Chavez nodded. The rapt expression on his face surprised me. I expected information like this about our patron saint to bore or even antagonize him.

"His father was a master at Rugby, the public school Rupert attended. The Brookes belonged to the upper middle class at a time when the British Empire was at its peak."

"Tell us about his mother," Jennifer said.

"Ah…the Ranee."

"Renee? That was her name?"

"No. One of Rupert's nicknames was 'the Rajah.' You know, like Maharajah, an Indian prince. Therefore, his mother became known as the Ranee, the Indian word for queen."

"Why did Rupert get that name in the first place" I asked. I was curious about nicknames because James had bestowed one on me – Ambele – without explaining why.

"I think there was some rumor he was related to a real Rajah named Brooke, an Englishman who went to India and conquered a kingdom. But the name probably stuck because Rupert was so princely."

"Because he had beauty of face," Chavez joked.

"Yes, face, body, intellect. The people who made him their prince went on to dominate British life. Maynard Keynes, Lytton Strachey, Virginia Stephens."

"Better known as Virginia Woolf," I added. "You're talking about the Bloomsbury group. Weren't they all conscientious objectors to World War I? I think they were all socialists or communists too, even though they all lived off of inherited incomes."

I felt uncomfortable with James's biography of public school boy Rupert Brooke. He was born privileged in a time and place of rigid class distinctions. He was born with blue eyes, blonde hair and a silver spoon. The hero of the Great Lovers was an aristocrat.

James must have read my mind.

"Don't worry, Tate. Rupert broke with Bloomsbury. That's why he was in America and why he went to the South Seas."

"So what happened at this building?" Chavez said.

"Rupert blew the socks off of stodgy old Boston, Chavez."

James was ebullient. He shook Chavez's shoulders.

"He passed through the city in his baggy English tweeds, with his ruddy athlete's cheeks, his cascading blond hair swept off his forehead, his slightly upturned nose and Boston saw...can you guess?"

"A Greek God?" From Jennifer.

"A lion?" Pugnacious Chavez.

"A poet?" Literal Rayna.

"And you, Tate. What do you think the employees of the *Atlantic Monthly* saw when Rupert Brooke walked up these steps and strode through the door there?"

"That he was doomed?"

"They beheld immortality."

An elegant elderly man walked out of the building. If he saw anything noteworthy in the five sailors standing on the steps, he didn't let on.

Halfway to Beacon Street, however, he turned and, I swear, stared at James like he had seen a ghost.

*

There is one other thing I want to tell you about Rupert today. You probably have already sensed this from the poem. He had a premonition of his future."

"That he would die young?" Chavez asked.

"Yes. And that Europe was destined for a catastrophic war."

We were at Harvard University when we had this discussion, standing around the statue of John Harvard.

"Rupert visited Harvard too in 1913. He crossed the Charles River to see the commencement exercises. There was a parade of alumni, arranged by class. It was a stream of men, young to old. Rupert noticed something strange, however. There seemed to be no one between fifty to sixty years old. Shaken, he asked a friend from Harvard about this. 'The War,' the friend answered solemnly. It was the first time he understood the losses the War Between the States inflicted. He later wrote a newspaper article about that hole in the parade."

"Do you think he was moved by this because he guessed the same thing was going to happen to his generation?" Jennifer asked.

"I do think that," James answered.

We had time for a quick bite to eat before catching the return bus. Faneuil Hall wasn't far from the station so we decided to chow there. The restaurant we could all agree on had a selection of oysters and clams on chipped ice. We all ordered clam chowder. James hesitated before dipping a spoon into his bowl.

"You know, Rupert didn't really like the food in Boston. They served clam chowder on the ship across the Atlantic and he thought it was the most revolting thing. For him, clam chowder stood for American vulgarity. Clams, potatoes, onions. But, I'm sorry, I just can't resist it. Or those clamcakes you get in Rhode Island."

James didn't, as he promised me, reveal his radical ideas on that trip to Boston. But I didn't have to wait much longer.

*

Finally, over brunch at an expensive hotel on Ocean Drive, James announced that it was time to discuss our principles.

"I had more in mind than guaranteeing your commissions when I started this nuclear family in the Navy family."

He looked closely at the faces of the other brunchers in the restaurant before continuing. Satisfied that there weren't any spies, he continued.

"We are going to transform the Navy!"

"Sure. When we make Admiral like your father. Until then we follow orders," said Chavez.

"Wrong. As soon as we become Ensigns we can start. Change won't happen overnight, but it has to begin somewhere."

"Wait a second, James," Rayna objected. "What is it you want us to achieve?"

"The ultimate, unbeatable military force, of course. The Navy buys the most sophisticated weapons and equipment in the world, but doesn't do anything to update its most valuable commodity. Us. The personnel. Does anybody have a pen?"

Jennifer found one in her purse.

"Cloth napkin, can't write on that," he muttered. Then he pulled an envelope out of his coat pocket. It was a letter he'd received that morning with a Martha's Vineyard return address. Admiral and Mrs. Drayton had retired out there.

James wrote on the back of the envelope:

"WHAT WE (THE GREAT LOVERS) BELIEVE

The distinction between officers and enlisted personnel should be eliminated."

Chavez stood when James read aloud the first principle of our society.

"You're crazy, James."

Rayna grabbed his hand. "Sit down, Chavez. People are looking."

He did as she asked, and it was at that moment I first realized they were lovers.

"I know what you're all thinking. Why go through OCS for that little gold bar on our collar when we're just going to eliminate rank? I don't expect you to agree with me right away, but I want you to consider the idea. The distinction between officer and enlisted restricts communication. Orders have to pass down a rigid chain of command. In the modern world we don't have time for a bunch of officers in a command center to mull over the situation like in a war game. We need fast action and fast words in an electronic war. We can't be slowed down by having to follow a chain of command."

"Somebody has to give orders," Jennifer said.

"We spend billions of dollars on defense in anticipation of the next big war. Nobody can predict what that war will be like. But I know one thing. Decisions are going to be made on the spot. Breaking down the formality and hierarchy can only help us be limber."

"So what else are we going to believe?" Rayna asked, resigned.

James wrote: "All sailors must be Great Lovers."

"That sounds terrible, James. They'll laugh us out of the Navy. It sounds soft," I said.

"Perfect. That's just what I wanted to hear. Soft, kind, warm and fuzzy, that's just what we're striving for."

"This is the military. We're warriors," Chavez growled.

"Rupert Brooke was a warrior. And a poet. And a decent man. He is the model of what a soldier should be. The words of 'The Great Lover' testify to his love of the earth. Tate, what is the current military philosophy when it comes to training?"

"Reduce us to a pulp and then build us back up again."

"That's right. They call it building character through adversity. Humiliation, sleep deprivation, physical punishments, enforced uniformity. Throw in a little coursework and that's how the Navy makes its members fit for service. There's only one word for this in today's world. Brutality. It's harmful and unnecessary and creates the kind of climate where these things happen."

He opened the envelope and removed a typed list, which he read aloud.

"Annapolis. The Naval Criminal Investigative Service concludes that over 80 midshipmen cheated on the exam for Electrical Engineering 311." This was the most minor of the items. The list also included horror stories about hazing rituals, allegations of sexual assault and battery at a convention of military members, beatings, and even killings, by soldiers against other soldiers or civilians motivated by hate.

There was silence after James concluded.

"You're talking about a handful of people," I said.

"Maybe. Or maybe these are just the most flagrant abuses, like the first symptoms of a horrible disease. I think if we want to win the next war, it's not going to be with the military I just described."

"Keep dreaming. You can't change the way soldiers have been trained for centuries," Chavez said.

"The five of us can start by working against prejudice, sexism and hazing wherever we see it."

"I agree with James," I said. "We need new ideals for the new ways of war."

"We're going to be late getting back to the base. Is there anything else, James?" Rayna asked.

He whispered something and wrote on the envelope.

"I didn't hear you," said Rayna.

James pushed the envelope across the table. We passed it around to see what he had written.

"Retaliation against those who are not Great Lovers."

I thought, "Ryan."

Later, after lights out, I asked James if his father had encouraged him to start the Great Lovers.

"Of course not. Why?"

"That list of crimes and abuses you read came in today's mail. I picked it up from the floor and put it on your desk. The return address was Martha's Vineyard. That's where your parents live."

"I don't want to talk about it."

"Are we the first Great Lovers or is this a secret society that has existed for a long time?"

"Believe me, Tate, we're the first group to be fighting for love within the military."

"Is retaliation love?"

"We'll retaliate only in self-defense."

"A real Great Lover would turn the other cheek."

James only laughed.

*

Our seniors hadn't abused us too badly, except for the first week when they woke us at three in the morning by banging on our doors and screaming fire. Once in a while they would destroy our room so we would have more of a mess to clean before inspection in the morning. The seniors weren't allowed to lay hands on an Indoc (the OCS word for plebe), but they could order sit-ups or push-ups for an infraction.

We would only remain Indocs until the winter break. After that, we would graduate to seniors and have our own class of Indocs to terrorize. The Great Lovers wouldn't haze them though...we would lead by love.

James warned us that we should expect trouble before the seniors passed the torch. An initiation. He warned us to keep our cool when it happened, despite our sworn opposition to needless cruelty. "All sailors must be Great Lovers. Retaliation against those who are not Great Lovers." That was our credo, but evidently we were to ignore it for the time being.

The lights came on at 0153. Pandemonium in the hallway. A senior ordered James and me out of our racks.

I started to put on my sweat suit.

"Nope. In your underwear," the senior said.

In the hall, another senior commanded the males to sit with our backs to the wall. The females were being led away by women seniors. I watched Jennifer and Rayna and the four other female Indocs in our Company march away. Jennifer looked back at James.

"At least they get to wear clothes," I whispered to James. "It's freezing out here."

"Stop shivering, Tate. They'll think you're afraid."

"I'm just cold."

39

"Everybody bump up. Pass it down," James said.

The eighteen Indocs huddled together for body warmth. I was still shivering. Maybe it wasn't only the cold.

From the corner of my eye, I saw that the seniors had set a table at the end of the corridor. Mulvey, our Company commander, lifted a carton of extra large eggs from the table.

"Good evening, bellringers," he drawled in a southern accent that always sounded a little thick, for a Texan, to me." He called us bellringers because the Master Chief in charge of our training was always inviting us to ring the bell he carried if we wanted to quit OCS.

"Good evening, sir," we barked.

"You thought it was smooth sailing now, didn't you?"

"No, sir."

"We're not going to graduate without leaving an impression on you, Indocs. We're thinking that we haven't tested you enough. Can't hand over control until we can be sure you're fit for it. So I've come up with some tests. The first is called 'the poached egg.' The rules are simple. All you have to do is pass an egg from mouth to mouth without breaking the yolk."

We laughed along with the seniors at the game rules. Maybe this wasn't going to be so bad.

"Laugh now, Indocs. You won't be laughing later."

He cracked an egg into an ashtray and slid it into the first mouth in line. James was eighth and I was ninth. The first yolk only stayed whole until the fourth person.

"Swallow that scrambled egg, Arnold," Mulvey ordered. "You're a bunch of hose-ups, aren't you?"

"Yes, sir!"

"Ruining a good egg like that. Get down and give me twenty."

We started the pushups, but then the Company commander ordered us to stop.

"I don't want you sweating in here until you apply a fresh coating of deodorant. Lift your arms."

The seniors, carrying jars of peanut butter, knelt among us and spread jiffy peanut butter under our armpits.

"NOW give me twenty."

After the punishment, we resumed the egg poaching exercise. It took eight attempts to get the yolk from one end of the line to the other. Each time the yolk broke we had to perform peanut butter pushups.

"I hope you are all done digesting your breakfast eggs because it's lunchtime now. What's on the menu today, Chef Tell?" Mulvey asked another senior.

"I do believe it's the peanut butter sandwich. Peanut butter and sweat on a week old onion bagel."

The Indoc to my right, Chang, started to heave.

"It's just talk," I whispered to him.

Down the line, Chavez sat with his eyes locked rigidly ahead. I guessed he had been through scenes like this before and knew that the best tactic was stoic acceptance.

"Who's talking?" Mulvey demanded.

I raised my hand.

"Officer Candidate Gunderson? What did you say to Mr. Chang?"

"I was just saying how glad I am I don't have a peanut allergy."

A few of the seniors were amused, until Mulvey glared at them. James and Chavez stared straight ahead. I was letting the whole company down.

Then something amazing happened. James stood and walked to the room he and I shared and slammed the door behind him.

Mulvey and the rest of the seniors ran after him. I heard a struggle. When I tried to go in there to help him, someone circled me with his arms from behind. It was Chavez.

"Why not?" I pleaded with him.

Before he could answer, the seniors emerged from my room, carrying James, and dropped him on the deck. He returned to his former spot along the wall.

Mulvey was still giving orders but he didn't sound as commanding as before.

"Get down and give me twenty," he squealed.

When we finished and returned to the wall, he told us to raise our arms. Carrying the bagel halves, he stopped in front of each of us and wiped the contents of our armpits onto the bagel.

He handed the abomination to the first Indoc in line and invited, "Take a bite and pass it on."

"Don't eat that!" James countermanded.

"What is your problem, Drayton?" Mulvey asked.

"What's the point of all this?"

"The point is that my class went through a hazing and so will yours."

"My class is going to pass on eating that bagel or doing anything else filthy, unhealthy or dangerous."

"Speak for yourself, Drayton," yelled one of the Indocs James was trying to protect.

"Why don't you just skip this and let us go to bed?" James pleaded. "You'll all be out of here in two days anyway."

"This is one of the jobs we have left before we go, and as company commander I'm going to see that we finish it."

"Who gave you the order to haze us? Who will you be disobeying if you refuse?"

"Nobody ordered me. It's a tradition. Hazing teaches you to stand up to stress, to hold on during a prisoner of war situation. I don't have to justify anything to you."

"You've been in the Navy four months, Mulvey. You're not even a commissioned officer yet. What do you know about combat stress or being a prisoner of war? Get real."

Mulvey kicked James in the stomach. James slumped forward.

"Are you crazy, Mulvey?" one of the seniors said.

I tended to the leader of the Great Lovers. I intended to protect him from any more blows. Mulvey was no longer a threat though. He was on his knees gasping for air. Chavez had repaid him for the injury to James. But now Chavez was in an unfair fight against a half dozen seniors.

I heard voices at the far end of the corridor. The females had returned from their separate hazing ritual.

Rayna screamed when she saw one Great Lover down and another losing a fight. She ran down the hall and fought for Chavez. Then I entered the fray, which made James's adrenaline flow. Nor could Jennifer stand by. Soon all the Great Lovers were battling.

None of the other Indocs helped us.

Mulvey called off the seniors. A good thing for us because we were outnumbered.

"Kiss the Navy goodbye, Drayton. I'm bringing you up on charges of insubordination and striking a superior officer. Same goes for Gunderson, Chavez, Levy and Washington."

"You're the one who can forget about a commission," James said. "You kicked me in front of dozens of people. You know you aren't allowed to touch an Indoc. In the morning I'm going to report you to the CO. I hope your parents aren't coming to see you graduate. Investigations take time. You're probably looking at another month before you get cleared or disenlisted. Probably DE'd."

"You started this mess, Drayton. I'm just doing what I'm supposed to. But you win. I'll stop the hazing and we'll forget this ever happened. Is that what you want?"

"I just want a better Navy."

James was now in control, and it was he who gave the order to return to our rooms.

*

One night when Ryan had Officer of the Deck duty, James risked another meeting in our room to continue the biography of the poet.

"After Rupert left Boston, he continued across the continent. When he reached San Francisco, he considered turning back to England. I'm glad he didn't. The finest period of his life – as a poet and as a man – began when he decided to continue his journey. He sailed to Hawaii, then to Samoa and Tahiti. He was happy and prolific on this journey because he had escaped."

"Escaped what?" Jennifer asked.

"I'll show you," he said.

He removed a slender volume from his locker. The spine held onto the cover by just a few threads.

"This is *Poems 1914* by...him."

All the Great Lovers extended their hands to the book. By then we knew by heart the poem from which we took our name. During classes I would roll Rupert's words around in my head to produce happy daydreams. I thirsted for more of Rupert Brooke and so apparently did everyone else. But James clutched the book.

"He wasn't escaping the success of this book by going to Tahiti, because it wasn't published until after his death. It was this he had to flee."

Careful hands spread the covers and pinched the top of a page that was thicker than the others. James turned the book around so we could see...a photograph of James?

James said, "This was the best selling volume of poetry of the century. Its success was due in large part to this portrait of Rupert taken by Sherril Schell in 1913 when Rupert was twenty six."

He gently removed the protective layer of onion paper and we saw him for the first time.

Rupert Brooke in bare-chested profile.

Long hair like I had before the Navy barber buzzed it.

Features as delicate as a woman's on a strong neck that was a man's.

"He travelled to the South Seas to escape the power of the face you see in this photo. People didn't treat him normally in England or in America. The sight of him made women, and men, babble about the Greek gods. Rupert encouraged this to a certain degree, but it also forced him to act a part. In the South Seas he could be a mere man. Another standard of beauty prevailed there. Rupert became just a strange pale face among all the dark ones. There he found freedom from the features nature had given him.

"He fell in love with a girl named Taata Mata. Rupert's biographers claimed she was a princess, but that seems to have been a lie.

"She nursed him through coral poisoning. And even though she was probably a prostitute attached to his hotel, her love for him was pure and not bought. In Tahiti, with Taata Mata as his muse, he wrote some of his best poetry, including 'The Great Lover.' But he couldn't stay forever."

"Why not?" Chavez asked. "Warm nights, beautiful women. Nothing would have dragged me away."

"Rupert was human. When he was in England he longed to escape it. When he left his country, he was homesick, sighed for it. He borrowed the money for a passage to San Francisco and eventually Great Britain."

That was the end of that installment of James's life story of Rupert Brooke.

*

When the others left that night, James took another book from his locker and sat at the end of my bed.

"Shall I tell you who you were, Ambele?"

"No, why don't you keep me in suspense for another hundred years."

"Ambele was Rupert's guide on his walking tours through Tahiti. In a letter, he described him as six feet high, very broad and more perfectly made than any man or statue he had ever seen."

"That's a ridiculous comparison, James. I'm only five eight, even if I am more perfectly made than any man or statue."

"The point is not physical resemblance. Ambele guided Rupert through Tahiti, carried him when he was weak or hurt, protected him. You're my bodyguard. The person I trust most in the world."

He put the book away, closed his locker and snapped off the light.

*

We walked single file through the woods with James leading the way. It was the day of our final examination – recitation of the poem from memory. Since "The Great Lover" described the love of nature, James decreed we would hold this meeting outdoors. The site he chose was a bird sanctuary.

Unfortunately, we still were not allowed to go off base in civilian clothes, and we marched in black dress shoes through the muck. James consulted a trail map and eventually led us up a rock. Rayna stumbled and caught my waist for support.

"I thought the Great Lovers were against hazing, James," I shouted.

"This builds character," he replied.

A spectacular view opened before us of the ocean.

We followed James up another rock even closer to the beach. There was now nothing between us and the Atlantic but a marsh full of ten foot high cattails and a thin margin of dunes. Upon this platform, though, nothing blocked the wind. It was impossible to hold a meeting up here.

James basked in the wind and sun while the rest of us huddled together.

"Is this it?" Jennifer asked.

"No. In the cave."

He jumped down the right side of the rock to a ledge four feet below. At the front of the rock, the ledge led into a protected mouth between upper and lower lips of stone. It was warm and quiet in the groove.

"This place is Hanging Rock. The first item of business is congratulations. A source in admin tells me that Chavez will graduate 20th in the class, Jennifer 21st, Rayna at number 30 and Tate at 32."

"And you, James?" Jennifer asked.

"First," he stated sadly. "I wish I could have brought the rest of your higher."

There was no question that all of us had benefitted from the society.

"I discovered Hanging Rock when my father taught at the Naval War College in Newport when I was in high school. I would ride my bike out here, look at the water, and wish I could join the Navy. That was also the summer I discovered Rupert Brooke's poems. Let me tell you about Rupert in the war. After he left Tahiti, he arrived in London in June 1914. By September, he received a commission in the Royal Naval Division and quickly saw action in Belgium. In February 1915, he departed with the British Mediterranean Expeditionary Force to liberate Constantinople. He never made it there. His body wasn't as strong as it looked. Maybe he hadn't recovered from the coral poisoning he came down with in Tahiti. In any case, he developed blood poisoning. On April 23, 1915 he died on a French hospital ship off the Greek island of Skyros. They buried him on a hill in Skyros, in a grave marked by a simple white cross. Britain knew immediately what she had lost – her greatest poet, her kindest heart, her finest man, who gladly gave his most precious gift, his life, to her."

James then began reciting "The Great Lover." After delivering the first ten lines, he nodded at Jennifer to continue. When she had recited for a time he stopped her and gestured at Chavez. Rayna was next, I last.

*

When we returned to the base, I learned that while we were taking the final exam of our course on Rupert Brooke at Hanging Rock, Ryan Morrissey was being questioned by agents of the Naval Criminal Investigative Service. Someone in our company told us this as soon as we returned to OCS. I was certain that Ryan was telling all he had surmised or overheard through the walls about the Great Lovers. Horrified, I looked at James.

"Ryan has some more pressing issues now," James said, in response to my fear.

Jennifer explained.

"Ryan's father owns a company that does construction for the military. That company was involved in some bid-rigging scandal. Ryan told me he worked at the company while this was going on. He claims he knew nothing about the criminal activities of his father. But he was afraid if the Navy ever found out, especially with his going into the Supply Corps...."

"He'd be dead," I said.

"It's been eating him since he got here. He had to confide in his new best friend."

"I wondered why you were so friendly with him. James told you to get the dirt."

"The idea came to both of us at the same time, right, James? Anyway, after Ryan confided in me, I felt it was my duty to inform the CO."

James said, "Unfortunately, I don't think Ryan will be graduating with us."

He smiled.

I expected all along for Ryan to pay for his nosiness. Intimidation or threats were what I envisioned. Having him kicked out of the school when he was so close to receiving a commission, that was too much.

"Don't look so concerned, Tate," James said. "Even Great Lovers have enemies."

PART TWO: COOL FLOWERS

With James and Jennifer in Norfolk attending intelligence school, Chavez in Newport at Surface Warfare Officer School and Rayna and I in Athens, Georgia at Supply Corps School, letters and phone calls had to replace meetings. Having received our commissions, we still weren't considered able to join the fleet – first we had to receive training for our specialty.

I missed Great Lover study sessions and outlines. Rayna and I sometimes crammed together, but it wasn't the same thing.

I awaited the instruction James was sure to send. Recruit. Form another cell of Great Lovers. After a month in Georgia, I finally asked him if I should find people who were likely to support the concepts of Great Love and a Navy without officers.

'No!" came his emphatic reply.

I didn't question him about it. In fact, I was happy our group remained so exclusive. James wrote a newsletter to all the Great Lovers and even some letters to me alone. From both sources I learned that he and Jennifer had rented a little beach house together. On-base housing was tight, so the Navy paid for them to live elsewhere. They spent weekends in D.C. and discovered Rupert Brooke material in the Library of Congress. Afterwards, they drank beer and ate barbecue in Georgetown.

I found myself jealously skipping over the details of their outings and then, my curiosity getting the better of me, pulling the letters out of their envelopes late at night to face the proof of their affection for each other.

Jennifer never even sent me a postcard.

James organized a reunion in Norfolk for Memorial Day. Rayna and I drove north in her Saab convertible. Chavez drove south in his truck. Finally, I could judge for myself how things stood between Jennifer and James.

"Chavez beat us to Norfolk," I remarked when we arrived at the beach house.

"It will be nice to see him," she said pleasantly.

"Long distance relationships are hard. It will be awkward at first, but then you'll find your groove."

"Very astute, Tate. You're right on top of things as usual."

I wondered if she and Chavez had split up. If so, Rayna never mentioned it. Then again, I only guessed they were dating from their body language and manner with one another at OCS. But neither had confirmed it.

Their silence was fine with me. I didn't want to hear how Rayna and Chavez had found great love within the Great Lovers, because I was bitter than Jennifer and I had not.

I embraced James and Chavez and nodded to Jennifer.

"Sweet place," I complimented them.

"We painted," Jennifer said.

"And we scavenged the furniture from the Salvation Army and flea markets," James added.

The pesto pasta with shrimp James prepared and the joy of reunion made us thirst for bottle after bottle of white wine. At midnight, when I suggested a swim, it seemed like the most sensible thing in the world.

"I didn't pack a bathing suit," Rayna said.

"Great Lovers don't wear clothes into the water, do they, James?" Chavez asked.

"Never."

It was high tide, and we didn't have to go far from shore before the water was chest deep.

"I'm freezing!" Jennifer complained.

"Get your hair wet and you'll feel better," Rayna told her. "I love this. All my impurities are being cleansed by the sea."

"You're reading too much Rupert," Chavez told her.

Chavez, Rayna and Jennifer swan further out while James and I lingered closer to the beach, body surfing. We rode the same wave in and ran back into the water to warm up. The temperature of the sea was more comfortable than the air.

I knew I had to act quickly, before the others made us join them.

"James" I asked in a low voice.

"What-o?' he replied in a loud one.

This had to happen quickly. "Come here." He moved closer. I grabbed his waist and kissed him. Then I backed off slightly. Just as I hoped, he reached for me. But as soon as his fingers brushed my arms I turned and swan out to the other Great Lovers. I thought it would feel better than it did to teach him what it was like to want something you can't have.

The next day, while the others slept off their hangovers, I found James outside on the deck, writing in a notebook.

"Homework?" I asked.

"No."

"Diary?"

"It's a letter to you, Tate. What were you thinking?"

"My brain tells me one thing about you and Jennifer – that you're best friends. Then there's this demon that sees the home you created together, hears the two of you saying 'we' all the time, watches you holding hands."

"You're in love with Jennifer," he said.

I must have known how foolish the idea was, because I walked away to avoid answering. It was raining, so the lifeguards had a day off. Their orange towers stood empty along the beach. I scrambled up the one behind James's shack, and he followed me soon afterwards. We sat together wordlessly.

We returned to the house. James picked up the notebook he'd been writing in and said, "I guess I don't have to finish this letter now. My head is pounding anyway."

If he had only thrown that letter in the ocean there would never have been any proof of the Great Lovers.

*

James owned a book of Rupert Brooke's letters, and on the second night of our reunion he read some of them to us. It bothered me that Rupert was a different person for each of the people he wrote to. Sometimes he was unbearably smug about his looks and talent as a poet, but writing to someone else he stressed that the most important thing in life was to be kind. About the war he could be flippant, but then he wrote with real seriousness about the danger he and his men would face. I have recently gone back to find the exact wording of one of the letters James read that afternoon, since it affected the subsequent course of my life so profoundly.

The passage appears in a letter to his lover Cathleen Nesbitt, an actress. He wrote on February 7, 1914 from Tahiti, where he had found a new lover. He asked her if she knew the significance in Tahiti of a flower worn over the right ear. It means that you are looking for a sweetheart. A white flower over the left ear means you have found a sweetheart, and a white flower over both ears means that you have a sweetheart but are searching for another. A flower over both ears was the height of fashion in Tahiti, he told Cathleen.

After the reading we dressed to go dancing. Jennifer and I actually danced together that night. She wore a denim shirt tucked into a white skirt that fell to her ankles. Since she wore sandals, I had to be careful not to mash her toes. Not that we got that close.

When I asked Rayna to dance, she declined but reached for my hand and pulled me outside. Chavez was hitting on a woman at the bar. Rayna must want to talk to me about that, I thought. Then I watched as she pulled a white flower from a tree by the pool and tucked it behind her right ear.

"Don't you remember what James said, Rayna. A white flower over the right ear means you're looking for a lover."

"Have I found one?"

"I don't know. Have you?"

She caressed my cheek with her knuckles. "You're the man I'm looking for tonight, Tate. I've wanted you to notice me for a long time."

"I thought you and Chavez were an item."

"That lasted two weeks. In case the white flower isn't an obvious enough invitation, I'm going to beg. Kiss me, Tate."

"Wait," I whispered.

I slipped the flower from her hair and placed it over my left ear.

"Kiss *me*, Rayna."

PART THREE: THE COURT MARTIAL

No charge or specification may be referred to a general court-martial for trial until a thorough and impartial investigation of all the matters set forth therein has been made. Article 32, Uniform Code of Military Justice.

I knew I was the last Great Lover to be questioned. Chavez, Rayna and Jennifer hadn't been in a tin can underwater. During the Article 32 investigation I had the right to counsel. He protected me from self-destruction, but couldn't tell me what my friends had already disclosed or had successfully kept hidden.

The questioning took place in New London, just hours after I learned of James's death. Numb.

"Who are the Great Lovers?" Commander Silver, the officer in charge of the inquiry, asked.

My JAG, Lt. Ahearn, nodded that I should answer.

"The Great Lovers was just the name of a study group that formed at Officer Candidate School," I admitted. "Once we graduated, we remained friends, and the name stuck."

"Did the Great Lovers have a code of conduct?"

"We were Navy officers. We subscribed to the Navy Code – we didn't lie, cheat or steal."

"You didn't hope to eradicate the distinction between officers and enlisted sailors?"

"We may have talked about it. Obviously, we ourselves were powerless to make a change like that."

"Were you and James Drayton lovers?"

"No."

"He made physical advances to you though?"

"Never."

"You kissed James once, didn't you, Ensign?"

"Are your satellites that good? I did give him a friendly kiss once."

"Were you and Rayna Washington lovers?"

"Yes."

"That upset Ensign Drayton, didn't it?"

"No. I think he arranged it. He told Rayna to put a white flower behind her ear which would mean...."

"Why did James make you the beneficiary of his life insurance policy?"

"We were best friends."

"Did you know that James Drayton intended to cause an explosion on the *Determination* to shame the Navy?"

"That's a lie. James was the greatest lover of the Navy there ever was."

"If so, then why did he feel the need to form a secret society to recreate the Navy in his own image?"

"I don't know."

My counsel never once said a word or cautioned me not to answer a question. I confronted him when the investigator left.

"If this goes to trial," I told him, "you're fired."

"It's going all right. And whether you desire my services or not, I'm still a superior commissioned officer. Address me as sir."

"Thanks for nothing, SIR."

*

From the questions asked during the Article 32 investigation I was able to predict the case the Navy would make.

A small group of unseasoned officers believes the Navy should change to suit the times. They call themselves the Great Lovers, yet they are haters of the centuries-old traditions of their service. These venerable customs stand firm against the Great Lovers' efforts at reform, so the Svengali of the secret society, James Drayton, resolves on another strategy.

During the Navy's most significant mission since the Gulf War, an intervention in the South China Sea to prevent a possible Chinese invasion of Taiwan, Drayton makes his move.

He sweets-talks his way into a part of his ship where he doesn't belong, the ammunition loading room. There he plants an explosive device in the place where it will cause the most damage. His own life and four others are lost. The carrier barely makes it to Japan, its mission incomplete. It will be several days before another carrier can arrive on the scene. Drayton and his Great Lover colleagues have succeeded. The Navy appears incompetent. The Great Lovers have sown the seeds of change but reaped human lives.

A catch in this theory...why would Ensign Drayton sacrifice himself. Quite easy to resolve actually. His obsession with a poet who died at twenty-seven required that he too make the "ultimate sacrifice" before reaching that age.

The Center for the Analysis of Violent Crimes at the FBI prepares a profile of Ensign Drayton. He was gay, and despondent because he was in love with a straight man, Tate Gunderson. Drayton was the insecure son of a powerful, dominant father and struggled in vain to surpass the achievements of the former Chief of Naval Operations. He was a loner with a secretive, conspiratorial bent. Generation X cynic and defeatist, he placed posters of Kurt Cobain and River Phoenix on his walls at college.

*

That was the government's case, as ridiculous and full of holes as it appeared to me. There was little physical evidence that James (or anyone) had planted an explosive device in the ammunition room. A hundred factors could have caused the ignition. There was even less evidence that the rest of the Great Lovers played any role in the events on the carrier. The Uniform Code of Military Justice, however, makes little distinction between mutiny by creating violence or disturbance and conspiracy to commit it. If James were guilty, the rest of us were culpable by plotting with him to change the Navy, for not turning him in initially when he revealed his seditious ideas.

The final report stated that the cause of the explosion could not be conclusively determined. Nonetheless, James Drayton and the Great Lovers had planned a mutiny, even if the disaster on the *Determination* was not it.

A general court-martial was recommended.

*

CHARGE I   Violation of the Uniform Code of Military Justice, Article 94(5), Failure to Report a Mutiny or Sedition.

SPECIFICATION   In that Ens. Tate Gunderson, Ens. Julius Cesar Chavez, Ens. Rayna Washington and Ens. Jennifer Levy did at Officer Candidate School and at their subsequent units or organizations fail to take all reasonable means to inform their superior commissioned officers or their commanders of a mutiny among the group called "The Great Lovers," of which mutiny they, the said Gunderson, Chavez, Washington and Levy, had reason to believe was taking place.

*

Getting court-martialed at least meant that the Great Lovers (minus the greatest) could meet again. As joint defendants we were allowed to coordinate our defense. Unfortunately, each of us had a government appointed lawyer attached, but we were in the same room.

Rayna had gained some weight from the inactivity and stress of the last several weeks. I stared at her left hand. The engagement ring was gone.

During the investigation, I found myself hating this secret society, its members, the person who created it and, especially, Rupert Brooke. The poet had captivated James, wrapped him in the myth of dying young and handsome. But my thoughts didn't always take that negative cast. Other times, I knew James had died in an accident, that he loved his friends, the Navy and life, and Rayna, Chavez, Jennifer and I would never again live as nobly as we did under his guidance.

I hoped that these fluctuations of feelings afflicted Rayna too and that she would not permanently despise the Great Lovers or me. At least my announcement would make her reconsider rejecting me.

"Before we begin, I want to announce that I have hired civilian counsel. It's someone famous who has never lost a case. Raoul Thomas," I boasted.

"The drummer?" Chavez asked.

"That's just his night job. He's even willing to miss a Tuesday night jam at Kevin's in New York to represent me -- us – at the court-martial."

Chavez's JAG Lawyer spoke up.

"He can't represent all of you. That would be a conflict of interest in a joint case like this."

"He already explained that to me. But he says getting me off is the same as doing it for everyone. He'll be lead counsel at the court-martial if the others agree."

"He's not coming to the trial with his beard tie-died again, is he?" Jennifer asked.

"That was just a stunt for the day Jerry Garcia died. He couldn't get away with those things if he weren't a great attorney."

"I don't know how I feel about this," Jennifer continued. "Don't you always have the feeling that the people he represents are guilty and are buying their way out of trouble? It will look bad to have him as a lawyer."

"We are guilty, Jennifer. We actually did form a secret society. We did swear to change the Navy. But Raoul says that was our right. Not only did he promise to try to deliver a not guilty verdict, he hopes to keep us all in the Navy."

"How are you paying for this?" Rayna asked.

"I'm using the money from James's insurance policy."

Our lawyers announced that the reunion was over, and that we had to help them prepare our defense. Afterwards, I wondered why we didn't hold a moment of silence for James, console each other for his death. We were so eager to give ourselves a future that James disappeared.

But no, that wasn't it. Together in that room we were the Great Lovers again and James, like Rupert Brooke, gained life from our convocation. He was there. That's why we didn't mourn him.

*

All of our defense meetings were held at the base in Norfolk, which is also where we were imprisoned. That's putting it a little strongly. I was confined to a cell and placed under guard only during my time in the submarine. Once I arrived in Groton and soon afterwards in Norfolk, where the rest of the Great Lovers had preceded me, my status was downgraded to arrest. I assumed a new job in which my murderous, mutinous impulses found no outlet: copy editor of the base newspaper. Occasionally I let a typo pass to satisfy my diabolical nature. Arrest meant that I had a moral obligation not to leave the base without permission or to board a ship. The worst part of the arrest agreement regarded meeting with Chavez, Rayna and Jennifer. We were only permitted to see each other for trial preparation, in the presence of our attorneys. No one dared associate with the black-listed sailors, so I made no new friends either.

Raoul Thomas flew down from New York in July just before the arraignment. His flight, hotel and meals were all expenses I would have to pay. We met him in a classroom of Centennial Building, which was ours until the trial commenced.

The room resembled a surgical theater. In the center sprawled a square table marked with white grid lines. A balcony with several rows of seats surrounded the table on three sides. Before the dawn of computers, instructors waged war games on the table below while junior officers gazed from above. Now, the real Navy had moved elsewhere, and the excuses and defenses of the Great Lovers flew across the table instead of mock battleships.

Raoul Thomas had lumbered into the room, mopping his forehead with a handkerchief the size of a catboat sail. He wore his trademark white suit. I estimated the jacket to be a size 48 or 50. Thomas looked as white and huge as the Abominable Snowman and, like that mystical creature, his natural element was the cold.

"The Great Lovers, I presume," he gasped.

We all stood upon his entry. Chavez opened a folding aluminum chair for our savior in white. Thomas eyed the seat a little suspiciously, waved Chavez away and sat on the table instead.

"I should have guessed from the name Centennial Building. No air conditioning in 1876, none now."

"So what's going on with our case?" Jennifer asked.

"I've been boning up on courts-martial," He boasted.

"You've never handled one?" Chavez asked.

"Dear me, no. Terribly exciting. I find new experiences so stimulating. They call the jury…it's on the tip of my tongue…."

"The members," Rayna told him.

"Are you smart as a whip! The fiancé?" he asked me.

"Not any more," Rayna said.

"If you don't have much – or any – experience in military courts, why don't we make one of the JAGS the main defense counsel. You can assist," Jennifer implored.

"How hard can it all be?" Thomas scoffed. "It's not even a real court."

"It's real to us," Chavez insisted.

"You're right, Mr. Chavez. The charges against you are real as this heat. In civilian life you would be guilty of nothing worse than elitism, like George Bush belonging to Skull and Bones. I think I can carry over the civilian picture of things by deliberately stumbling over the rules of the court-martial. That's why I am appearing not to have mastered them."

"Why did you take this case, anyway?" Rayna asked.

"It's not only the money. I turn down dozens of cases every week. Have you read my autobiography *A Hunger For Justice*?"

"No. Are you still hungry?" she asked, glancing at the stomach that overhung the meaty shanks.

"Famished. I guess you Great Lovers haven't moved beyond Rupert Brooke on your reading list. My pride is hurt."

Even I hadn't read his autobiography, although I remembered the cover. Raoul Thomas, bathed in purple light, playing drums at Kevin's in New York. Sweat ran down his face and bliss shut his eyes. "Music is justice, justice is music," was Thomas's famous motto, and the photo captured that equation.

"Read Chapter Two – 'Taps.' It tells the story of why I decided to go to law school. Hell, it's the story of my own court-martial. In 1968, Second Lieutenant Raoul Thomas of the Marines attended an off base rally. I carried a sign that read, 'Johnson is a facist! U.S. out of Vietnam.'"

"What's a 'facist?'" I asked.

"I misspelled fascist. At first that embarrassed me more than being photographed by military police. I was out of uniform, incidentally. They court-martialed me for conduct unbecoming an officer and a gentleman, good old Article 133. The government wanted a year of hard labor, loss of pay and a discharge. My attorney argued that speech at a rally was protected by the First Amendment. I didn't even speak, just carried a piece of poster board that advertised that I couldn't spell. The members of my general court-martial considered my finger painting on cardboard a clear and present danger to the security of the armed forces."

"You know all about military law then," I said.

"Yes. I just wanted to give you a preview of my strategy. I'm playing the jackass civilian attorney who stumbles over all the hallowed military traditions."

"What will that accomplish, other than making the members pity us for having a fool for a lawyer?" Chavez asked.

"Does the term 'Trojan Horse' mean anything to your generation other than a rubber? The trial counsel is going to let down her guard and consider her case won when out of this big white horse will emerge the tightest, meanest military lawyer she's ever seen."

"She?" Jennifer asked.

He removed a thick file from his briefcase and searched for something.

"Here it is. Lieutenant Commander Christina Brandt. She has an endearing signature. The 'C' looks like a smiley face."

"Maybe she's planning a Trojan Horse of her own," Jennifer observed.

"I've spoken to her a few times on the phone after I've intentionally fouled up some procedure or other. She thinks she's holding my hand through this. Wait until I bite it off! We'll all see her tomorrow at the arraignment."

I began to think I chose wisely by hiring this man. After the meeting broke up, I bought his book and one other – *The Caine Mutiny*.

*

Thomas carried a large plastic shopping bag with him into the courtroom. When I asked him what was inside, he merely smirked and said, "I'm not telling, but it's made in America."

When we and our four assistant defense counsel were all seated, Thomas revealed what he had brought. It was a three-speed revolving fan, assembly required. It was still only a heap of parts spread across the table when LCDR Brandt, the trial counsel (or prosecutor in civilian language), entered with her own assistant. It would take one of those hard-boiled detective novelists of the Raymond Chandler variety to describe Christina Brandt. Legs ups to her eyebrows, cheekbones out to her shoulders, killerbee-stung lips. After four months in a submarine and another two in one kind of confinement or another, I was hornier than a New York City traffic jam. It was stupid to lust after my enemy, though.

Rayna nudged me, the first positive sign in weeks, and ordered, "Help him put that piece of crap together."

It didn't take me long. Thomas was just not mechanically minded, or pretending not to be. Grunting and cussing, he knelt and plugged the fan into a wall outlet, and it soon upset everything not nailed down in the courtroom. It bothered the trial counsel's equanimity, but not her tightly pinned red hair. She glared at Thomas, but didn't ask him for an explanation. I'm sure she wanted to see what the judge would make of this.

We stood when he entered. The fan attracted his notice immediately.

The military judge, Captain Al Eagleeye, though in his fifties, was compact and powerfully built, like a trapeze artist. He had a head of thick black hair, without a trace of silver in it.

Raoul Thomas stood. "Your honor, may I explain the presence of this American-made rotary cooling device on my desk?"

"I wish you would."

"I don't function in the heat. My clients and I met yesterday in the Centennial Building on this base. On the third floor of that noble edifice, bearing a plaque from the National Register of Hot – pardon – Historic Places, we discussed the charge. Heat rises, your honor. The heat induces in Southerners stillness, alcoholism and literary talent. If I am forced to continue to meet my clients in the infernal conditions of that stifling third floor room, I may start drinking and writing like Faulkner, but I will be unable to practice law. I heard the court might be as uncomfortable as that war room, so I brought a fan."

"Are you asking for another conference room?"

"A cool one, I beg you."

"Trial counsel, please see to it."

"Yes, sir."

"The climate in here is quite comfortable by my judgment, Mr. Thomas. If you remove that fan from your desk, the accused will be arraigned."

*

LCDR Brandt stood and said, "All parties and the military judge have been furnished with a copy of the charges and specifications. Do the accused want them read?"

Reading from a script, Thomas bellowed, "The accused waive the reading of the charges."

The judge said, "The reading may be omitted."

Brandt continued, "The charges are signed by Admiral William Johnson, Commander, Pacific Fleet, a person subject to the Code as accuser. They are properly sworn to before a commissioned offer of the armed forces authorized to administer oaths, and are properly referred to this court-martial for trial by the Secretary of the Navy, the Convening Authority."

"How do you plead?" the judge asked.

Thomas stood for us. "Ensigns Gunderson, Chavez, Levy and Washington plead absolutely not guilty."

"This court-martial will convene with members on Monday at 0900," Eagleeye announced and left the room. LCDR Brandt followed him through the same door.

"You might as well keep the fan," Thomas told me. "You paid for it, after all."

Six days remained before trial and the man was still making lame jokes.

*

0900 MONDAY

Christina Brandt announced, "The prosecution is ready to proceed with the trial in the case of United States v. Chavez, Gunderson, Levy and Washington," she looked over at us, "who are present."

Captain Eagleeye gestured to the eight stern looking officers, five men and three women, who composed our jury.

"The members will now be sworn."

Trial counsel stood and read the oath.

"Do you affirm that you will answer truthfully the questions concerning whether you should serve as a member of this court-martial; that you will faithfully and impartially try, according to the evidence, your conscience, and the laws applicable to trials by court-martial, the case of the accused now before this court; and that you will not disclose or discover the vote or opinion of any particular member of the court-martial upon the findings or sentence unless required to do so in due course of law?"

Each member swore the oath, which took a good half hour. Captain Eaggleye then made it official. "The court-martial is assembled."

Thomas had previously explained to us that jury selection did not really exist in a court-martial. The Navy selects the members and we get stuck with their choices. Even so, there was an opportunity for *voir dire* of the members. Written questionnaires were distributed to the members, asking dates of birth, sex, race, marital status, sex, age and number of children, home of record, education, unit to which assigned, past duty assignments, awards and decorations received, and whether the member acted as accuser in any past court-martial. Thomas barely glanced at the members' written responses. The trial counsel didn't challenge any of the members, nor did he. At this stage, the challenge could only be for cause. But each side also received one peremptory challenge. In other words, we and Ms. Brandt, could throw one of the members out without having to give a reason.

"Will you exercise a peremptory challenge, Commander Brandt?" the judge inquired.

It was in the favor of the Great Lovers to have a young group of members. As expected, Brandt dismissed the youngest woman, presumably the most sympathetic to us of the group. At his turn, Thomas dismissed one of the two oldest men, the one with a wife and four grown children. That left as the most senior member, called the president of the court-martial, a fifty-seven year old Captain in the medical corps, who had never been married. Six members remained of the original eight. Only five were required for a general court-martial to go forward. I would come to know all the members' faces well during the trial, but at that moment I had a more pressing concern than searching for sympathy in the creases of foreheads or the set of mouths. The prosecution was about to call its first witness. His name was Ryan Morrissey.

*

1100 MONDAY/ WITNESS FOR THE PROSECUTION: RYAN MORRISSEY

Longer hair and a decent blue suit gave Ryan a better appearance that he had at OCS, but he still resembled a rabbit. His gut advertised lots of civilian pizza and beer.

He ogled Ms. Brandt as she asked him, "Do you solemnly swear that the evidence you shall give is the truth, the whole truth and nothing but the truth?"

"I swear," he promised in his shrill voice.

"Please state your name and address for the record."

"My name is Ryan Morrissey. I reside at 6910 Iguana Drive, Tampa, Florida."

"What is your occupation?"

"I sell used cars. But I'm honest," he assured the trial counsel. She tried not to look disgusted, because this was her witness on the stand.

"How were you occupied between the months of October and March two years ago?"

"I was an officer candidate at OCS in Newport, Rhode Island."

"Were you acquainted with the accused there?"

"They were all in my Company. Yes, ma'am."

"Would you characterize yourself as a friend of theirs?"

"No. They and James Drayton kept to themselves."

"So the accused were part of a clique at OCS, and you didn't belong to it?"

"What's a click?"

"A group, a band, a company within the company."

'Yes, they were a group."

"Did everyone notice this? Were they very obvious about preferring each other's company?"

"Not at all. They were very secretive. I think I was the only one who knew about them."

"Why you?"

"Well, I roomed next door to James and Tate. I mean Ensign Gunderson and Ensign Drayton, who is dead now. Our class had only been at OCS a week or two when I started hearing voices, a lot of them, after lights out. There were female voices too, so I was kind of curious about what was going on. One night I decided to just walk in on them."

"What did you find there?"

"All five of the Great Lovers, as the people on TV have been calling them."

"The defense objects to the witness's use of the term 'Great Lovers.'"

The judge questioned Ryan.

"Why do you call them that name?"

"That's what I heard they call themselves. I read it in the newspaper after the explosion."

"Did you ever hear them use that name?"

"No, sir."

"Objection sustained. Don't use that name for the accused, Mr. Morrissey."

Brandt continued. "Who exactly did you see in the room that night?"

"Chavez, Gunderson, Drayton, Levy and Washington."

"Did you speak to them?"

Ryan scratched his chin to aid memory. I noticed he was married now.

"I asked what they were always meeting for. They said it was a study group, and I couldn't join. But I didn't believe them about studying."

"Did you observe anything that made you believe this was anything other than a study group?"

"They all had great grades, so I believed they studied together. But there weren't any books open in James and Tate's room that night. And then there's something stranger. They never met in there anymore after I walked in on them. It was only when they acted so scared that I began to think they were doing something wrong."

"How do you know they continued to meet at all?"

"I was curious and followed them off the base a few times. They met at restaurants in Newport."

"No further questions."

*

Both Thomas and Brandt knew the role Jennifer played in alerting the NCIS to the illegal activities of Ryan's father. But neither attorney wanted to touch the issue. Thomas thought it made the Great Lovers look vindictive – arranging the discharge of the one person who knew of our existence. Brandt didn't want her witness's testimony to seem like sour grapes, revenge for Jennifer's getting Ryan disenrolled from the training course. Since the trial counsel skirted the issue, I expected Thomas not to cross-examine, so the point would disappear altogether. Ryan hadn't done us much harm. He merely stated that we met sometimes. Better to leave him alone.

Our lawyer stood.

"Mr. Morrissey, why didn't you graduate from OCS?"

Ryan glared at Jennifer.

"My father did construction for the military in Florida. He was convicted of bid-rigging to get a contract. I worked for his company back then. The Navy found out when they processed my security clearance."

"No further questions."

Thomas smiled at Christina Brandt. The Trojan Horse just let out a warrior. He had made Ryan admit that he was a security risk, without bringing Jennifer into the picture. The trial counsel could have drawn him out on the circumstances but, with a witness like Ryan, she judged she should just staunch the injury and proceed no further.

*

1400 MONDAY/ WITNESS FOR THE PROSECUTION: LT. PHILIP BARONNE

After lunch, the prosecution called as its next witness Lt. Philip Baronne. Brandt swore him in and asked, "Are you Philip Baronne, Lieutenant, United States Navy, attached to the aircraft carrier *U.S.S. Determination*?"

"Yes, ma'am."

"Do you know the accused?"

"No, I do not."

"Did you know Ensign Drayton?"

"Yes, ma'am."

Lt. Baronne was one of the men who escorted James to the hospital ship after the explosion. I thought he was a friend of James's and didn't understand his presence as a witness for the prosecution. Baronne was balding and scholarly looking.

"Lt. Baronne, what was your relationship with Ensign Drayton?"

"Shipmates first. I took him under my wing when he arrived on *Determination* as intelligence officer. It didn't take long for us to become friends. We went to shore together in Italy and southern

France. James knew a lot about painting and architecture. He was good with languages too. In other words, just the kind of person you want to travel with."

"Did you know Drayton was gay?"

"He was a little...."

"A little what?" Brandt asked.

"The word we used back in Wisconsin where I grew up is sensitive. He read poetry and would rather look at a statue than a person. He never came out to me though."

"Where were you last May?"

"On the *Determination*, near Taiwan, monitoring the Chinese missile exercises."

"What was your job on the *Determination* then?"

"Same as now. I'm a flyer."

"Did Ensign Drayton share his opinions of that mission with you?"

"He said this was typical of the Navy's role in the world today. A carrier battle group just had to show up to calm everybody down. Then he said something funny."

"Excuse me, when did this discussion occur?" his interrogator asked.

"Just a few days before the explosion that killed James."

"You characterized something Drayton said to you as funny. What was that?'

"I was reading this book by Patrick O'Brian. He writes historical novels about the English Navy during the Napoleonic wars. James had read the whole series. He asked me if I noticed that navies were still run like they were in the eighteen hundreds. I told him I thought that was great. I like that tradition."

"What did he say to that?'

"He disagreed. He believed we should update the structure of the Navy. I asked what in particular he would change. He said he would like to get rid of the officer-enlisted distinction and just have one system of rank. He also said he wanted to do away with all kinds of hazing and abusiveness in training."

"How did you respond, Lieutenant?"

"I told him it could never happen. He almost managed to change my mind though. I don't remember all his arguments now, but they were good. Society is changing and less willing to support a military if it lags behind the rest of America in tolerance. He gave me a rundown on some recent scandals and said that a few more embarrassments would force the Navy to change for good."

"Did he ask you to help him with his reforms?"

"He said that people with foresight would take control of the Navy someday. He asked if I wanted to be one of those people. I told him I was a conservative. He laughed and said he had changed other people's minds and would change mine too. That night he slipped a copy of a poem under my door. It was called 'The Great Lover.'"

"Did you read it?"

"Not until after James died. I have to admit I couldn't get much sense out of it."

"Did you tell your CO about James's ideas?'

"Only after the explosion."

"Why did you talk to him about this conversation you had with your friend?"

"I was afraid that the explosion was the embarrassment James had talked about that would make the Navy change."

"No further questions."

The military judge invited Thomas to cross-examine.

"I think I will, your honor," he said.

"I've asked you several times to call me Captain or sir, Mr. Thomas," Eagleeye warned. "This is a military court."

"A thousand pardons, your...sir."

"Proceed."

"Good afternoon, Lt. Baronne."

"Good afternoon, sir."

"Why didn't you tell your commanding officer about the conversation immediately?"

"At the time it was all just talk. And James was always giving me stuff to read."

"Have you ever discussed the topic of don't ask, don't tell with other officers?"

"Objection," Ms. Brandt fumed. "Ensign Drayton is on trial here, not Lt. Baronne."

"Captain Eagleeye, Ensign Drayton most assuredly is not on trial. Those men and women seated there are the ones waiting for the sound of justice."

"What is the relevance of your line of questioning, Mr. Thomas?"

"The witness described the alleged beliefs of ensign Drayton as 'funny' and potentially mutinous. I am trying to develop the difference between speech that is mutinous and that which is just conversation."

"You may answer the question, Lt. Baronne."

"Did I ever talk about gays in the military. Sure. I was at the Naval Academy when President Clinton was elected and promised to open up the military. Hardly anyone I knew supported him in that. Some midshipmen said they would kill any homosexual who came onto them. A couple said they would leave the military if Clinton succeeded with his plan."

"And what did you say during these conversations, Lt. Baronne?"

"I just listened."

"Like you listened to Ensign Drayton?'

"Yes, sir."

"Did you report the midshipmen who threatened violence or to refuse orders to your superintendent?"

"I did not."

"But they were expressing opinions that defied the wishes of the commander-in-chief elect?"

"It was their right to express their opinion. Freedom of speech applied. Freedom of religion too."

"Did freedom of speech apply when James Drayton told you his hopes for the Navy?"

"Objection. Lt. Baronne is not a Constitutional scholar."

"Lt. Baronne brought up the notion of freedom of speech," Thomas argued to the military judge. "I am merely trying to understand whether Ensign Drayton's pitch crossed the boundary into something more dangerous than stating an opinion, according to the witness."

"At the time I didn't think it crossed a boundary."

"One last question, Lieutenant. Are you familiar with Article 88?'

"No. I'm not a JAG, sir."

"Article 88 prohibits commissioned officers from using contemptuous words against the president or military departments. Did some of your friends at the academy use contemptuous words against President Clinton because of his opinion on lifting the ban against gay and lesbian service members?"

"Yes, they did, sir. I knew it was wrong, but I didn't speak up." He banged his knees with his fists.

"That's understandable. Ratting on a friend is one of the worst things you can do in the military, isn't it?"

"Yes."

"The truth is, Lt. Baronne, there is a lot criticism of the Navy and the government among your fellow officers, isn't there?'

"Yes, sir."

"No further questions," Thomas announced to Baronne's relief.

The judge had a question for the witness, however.

"Was Ensign Drayton well liked in the wardroom?"

"No. He was too much of a striker, too energetic. He made other junior officers look bad because he moved mountains on a daily basis. In time he probably would have settled down and grown as exhausted as the rest of us. If he hadn't kept so active, though, some officers would have accused him of getting by on his father's reputation. It was a no win situation for him."

"Thank you, Lt. Baronne. You are excused and free to go. As long as this trial continues, do not discuss your testimony or knowledge of this case with anyone except counsel. If anyone else tries to talk to you about the case, stop them and report the matter to me."

*

0900   TUESDAY/   WITNESS   FOR   THE   PROSECUTION: PROFESSOR PAULA CALAMARI

"The government calls Dr. Paula Calamari."

After Ms. Brandt opened the session with these words, the orderly left the room and returned with a short but powerful looking woman. She was a cross between a feisty Italian grandmother and a punk rocker. No effort had been made to disguise the fact that she had gone gray, but she cut her silver fox tresses into asymmetrical spikes. She wore a black Armani pantsuit and a black leather jacket.

I wondered again about a remark Thomas had made several weeks before. Did the trial counsel understand that she had hired as expert witness the academic world's most belligerent bigmouth, who claimed to be in love with Elizabeth Taylor one day and with Tom Cruise the next, who wrote articles comparing the lyrics of the Material Girl to the poems of the Belle of Amherst?

After she was sworn in, she was asked by Ms. Brandt to identify herself.

"Paula Calamari, Ph.D., Professor of English, St. Brigid's College, Trenton, New Jersey."

"Would you state for the court your educational background?"

"I have a bachelor's degree from Columbia University and my master's and doctorate from Berkeley."

"And do you have a specialty within the field of English literature?"

"I teach and write on my many subjects. I love pop culture. But I suppose British poets of the early Twentieth Century are my particular forte. I wrote my dissertation on the reputation of Rupert Brooke."

"Please tell the court who Rupert Brooke is."

Dr. Calamari looked at Ms. Brandt as if she were an unprepared student at St. Brigid's.

"He was a British poet who died in the Great War."

"The Great War being the scholar's term for World War I?"

"Everybody called it the Great War before World War II."

"You wrote your dissertation on the 'reputation' of this poet. That would seem to be a simple question. He was a good poet, or a bad one, right?"

"It's vastly more complicated than that. For one thing, Brooke died at such a young age that he did not leave a very large body of work. So the question is more than just whether he was talented or not. It is also what kind of poet would he have become if he hadn't died in 1915."

"What was his reputation when he died?"

"I tell my students that in the years following his death, Brooke was as celebrated as all four Beatles put together."

"Isn't it rare for a poet to enjoy that kind of fame?"

"Now? Forget about it. There were a couple of reasons for his unusually large following. He was gorgeous. That's the main one. He wrote poems that were patriotic and easy to understand. And he died like a hero. England's wars had always been fought by a professional military prior to this. Never before the Great War had soldiers from all walks of life fought in battle and never before had so many young men died. Somehow Brooke's poetry helped Britain to come to terms with the war. A hero was needed and Brooke was it."

"How did his reputation change over time?"

"Although books of his poetry continued to sell, some people began to poke holes in both his life and his poetry."

"Why?"

"Well, he didn't actually experience much of the war. He died of blood poisoning we think, from a mosquito bite, and not from a German shell. Or he died of a venereal disease. He never experienced the horror of trench warfare. His poetry also seems to many rather precious. He writes about the joy of self-sacrifice, like war is a picnic. The language is incredibly removed from the real experience of battle."

"Can you give me an example of that kind of language."

"He called blood 'the red sweet wine of youth.'"

"As an expert, what is the best you can say about this poet as a soldier?"

"He was among the first to enlist and among the first to die. His poetry gave courage to other soldiers fighting a brutal war and solace to relatives and friends of a generation of the dead."

"Then you might even say that Rupert Brooke helped Great Britain and its ally the United States to win the war?"

"Yes, you could say that."

"Now the other side of the coin. What is the worst you can say about Rupert Brooke? I'm not talking here about the quality of his poetry but about his influence during the war."

Professor Calamari took a deep breath and stared at the ceiling. I think she liked Rupert too and didn't want to remove him from his pedestal. If she didn't idolize him, how could she have spent so much time on him?

"The worst about Rupert is as valid is the best. He was a kind of pied piper, used by the old men of Britain to lead its youth to slaughter."

"But in this case the pied piper disappeared as well," the judge added.

'It's sad," the professor said. "Rupert Brooke was so fragile he didn't even make it to the real war in order to die there."

"How would you yourself characterize him?" Brandt asked.

"I think he wrote some superlative poems. The war poetry, however, is dangerously blind. And there was a homophobic and anti-Semitic element to him as well. I believe he left Britain for the South Seas because his prejudices got to be too strong."

"What if I told you there was a group in the military who worshipped Rupert Brooke. Would this concern you?"

Thomas awakened. "Objection, your honor, I mean, Captain. Dr. Calamari is not qualified to assess the United States Armed Forces."

"Objection sustained."

"Let me ask you a different question then, Professor. Has Rupert Brooke attracted hero worshippers?"

"Certainly."

"Why?"

"Again, his looks first and foremost. Perhaps the poetry. A myth of the saintly gentleman warrior was created after his death and protected by the guard dogs of his letters and papers."

"Is it only scholars who know about Brooke's alleged homophobia and anti-Semitism?"

"No, it's a tendency that is mentioned in all the recent biographies."

"So if James Drayton read a biography of Brooke, he would know that his hero poet hated men like himself?"

"Yes."

"No more questions."

Thomas rose.

"Professor Calamari, are you familiar with a poem by Rupert Brooke called 'The Great Lover?'"

"Yes."

"Forgive me if I stumble a little in my questioning. I've never found myself engaging in literary criticism before during a trial. I believe you characterized Brooke's poetry into two types. The red sweet blood of youth variety about warfare, and the other class, which is not war poetry, but about all the subjects poets explore: love, death, nature. Did I understand you correctly?'

"Yes. You must have majored in English."

"Philosophy. Now which category does the poem 'The Great Lover' fall into?"

'It's not a war poem, but it could...."

"It's not a war poem, you say. When was it written?"

"1913."

"There we go. It can't be a war poem because World War I didn't begin until 1914. I minored in history. No more questions."

Dr. Calamari looked a little uncertain as she left about what testifying against us would do for her own reputation.

*

1100 TUESDAY/ WITNESS FOR THE DEFENSE: ADMIRAL MICHAEL DRAYTON

Paula Calamari was the prosecution's last witness. Now it was our turn.

"The defense calls as its first witness Admiral Michael Drayton."

After the Admiral entered and the trial counsel administered the oath to him, Judge Eagleeye greeted the distinguished witness.

"Admiral Drayton, I sympathize with your loss. I know how painful a summons to this court must have been for you."

Admiral Drayton was an unwilling witness for the defense. Only a subpoena compelled him to come.

Thomas stood very close to the Admiral and requested he state his name and address.

"Michael Drayton, Admiral, United States Navy, Retired. I live on Oyster Lane in Martha's Vineyard, Massachusetts."

"Good morning, Admiral Drayton. Thank you for coming to Norfolk in this heat."

Admiral Drayton merely blinked. It wasn't a question, so he gave no response. Although it was on my recommendation the former CNO had been called, I feared his testimony could harm as much as help us. I knew very little about James's relationship with his father. That I

86

knew so little perhaps told everything. They were alienated, uninvolved with each other on a daily basis. Yet, they were so deeply connected that James followed his father into his profession and judged all his accomplishments against the old man's.

"Admiral Drayton, quite simply, did you know of the existence of a secret society called the Great Lovers?"

"No."

"Did you encourage your son to form a secret society to change the Navy?"

"No, I did not."

"Have you ever been a member of a secret society in the Navy?"

"No. I answered all of these questions during the Article 32 investigation."

"Did you correspond with your son while he was at Officer Candidate School?"

"I sent him two or three letters. He wasn't there long. Just four months."

"At any time in your correspondence, did you write to him about a cheating scandal at the Naval Academy and other scandals involving the military?"

"I wrote to my son about a rough ferry crossing, about the death of his cat Cathleen and about the success of some investments I had made for him. I also forwarded some magazines and letters that came for him on the Vineyard."

Thomas looked at me. I was certain James's father had compiled the list of abuses James had read to us. I had placed the envelope it came from on James's desk and noticed the return address belonged to his parents. Later that evening at our meeting, James read from the list and announced the core beliefs of the Great Lovers. Thomas and I drew two conclusions from this. Either a group of Great Lovers, counting the Admiral as a member, had long existed in the Navy and we were just the latest members, or the Admiral, impotent in his retirement, encouraged James to start the group. Both conclusions served to exonerate us. If the group was a long standing organization, or if Admiral Drayton had masterminded it, how bad could it be? He was one of the most decorated sailors alive and no one could doubt his loyalty. Nothing associated with him could be mutinous.

It was a risky gambit for Thomas to question him so directly about this on the stand, but I was certain James's father was responsible for his son's mission.

How could he lie under oath like this?

"Did you or did you not send a typewritten list of abuses committed by military personnel to your son?" Thomas tried again.

"I don't know how many times you want me to deny this. I've started to question my own memory of events. But this is the first time you've used the word 'typewritten' in connection with this alleged communication."

Gesturing to the stenographer, the Admiral continued, "I've been watching this able young man in amazement, because the ability to type has always eluded me. Maybe my generation of officers was spoiled, but I've never used a typewriter or computer in my life."

He was a convincing liar. The letter was typewritten, though, and I knew he typed it.

Ms. Brandt stood and registered her objection to this fruitless line of questioning.

"Captain Eagleeye, how much longer is this badgering of Admiral Drayton going to continue? Obviously, this letter which the defense wants to prove exists, for whatever reason, no longer exists or they would produce it. The Admiral didn't write it, has no knowledge of it, allow him to step down."

Suddenly the Admiral's face lost its aspect of firm, calm denial. Although I saw a rugged man with military bearing, at the same time I saw the pink-rimmed eyes and fear of abandonment of an infant. Admiral Drayton was looking at someone behind me. I distinctly saw him mouth the words, "My God." I turned around. A woman was standing.

"I wrote that letter," she said. "Leave my husband alone."

How could I have been so stupid? It was James's mother.

*

"Your honor, judge, Captain," Thomas sputtered. "The defense requests a recess."

The military judge agreed. He told Admiral Drayton he was temporarily excused and announced that the trial would resume at 1400.

In our conference room, Chavez said, "This isn't good. If the Admiral convinced James to start the Great Lovers, it's one thing. If it's his wife, and he doesn't even know about it, it reeks of revenge or sour grapes or something."

Thomas disagreed. "She had a job alongside her husband for forty years. Why couldn't she have developed some ideas of her own in all that time."

"But why didn't she tell her husband about it?' Rayna asked.

"Her husband couldn't even handle the fact that their son was gay. James and his mother kept that fact a secret," Jennifer said.

She was the only one of the Great Lovers privy to that information.

Thomas said, "We don't have much choice after that scene in there. Mrs. Drayton is going to have to explain herself."

As we ate our sandwiches, I reached for Rayna's hand. She didn't pull away, and we both ate our sandwiches one-handed.

On our way back to the courtroom, we walked past and saluted another young officer. Chavez yelled, "Hey, Chuckie!"

"Banana man!" the Lieutenant greeted him.

It was a friend of Chavez's from a ship he had served on. The nickname undoubtedly came from something that had happened aboard. Right there. That's when I most feared that this court-martial would prevent me from serving in the Navy again, because it was the instant I most missed it. Chuckie and Chavez shared a bond as intimate and rare as husband and wife, one which I too had known once: they were shipmates.

*

1400 TUESDAY/ WITNESS FOR THE DEFENSE: JILL DRAYTON

"The court-martial will come to order," the judge announced with a stern eye on Thomas. A former CNO sat on a plastic chair in the waiting room with his wife, also bound to be called as a witness, beside him. They had outlived a child and merited sympathy, no matter what their dead son had done.

Brandt said, "The members, the parties and the military judge are all present."

Admiral Drayton returned to the stand, but Thomas had no more questions. The trial counsel also did not wish to cross examine him, so he was dismissed as a witness.

"The defense calls Jill Drayton," Thomas thundered.

The judge looked at him like he thought Thomas was making a mistake or a joke. His tight smile disappeared when Mrs. Drayton entered.

Thomas asked her to please state her name and address.

"Jill Drayton, Oyster Lane, Martha's Vineyard, Massachusetts."

"Mrs. Drayton, do you know the accused?"

"Why, yes."

"Please point to each of the accused, stating his or her name."

Flawlessly, she indentified each of us, although we hadn't met her before. "I know them because my son described them to me. He had a gift for words and friendship."

"What is your occupation, Mrs. Drayton?"

"I'm a gardener. I sell plants and herbs on an honor system from my house. Customers leave the money in a jar. The money supports preservation projects on the island."

I guessed Jill Drayton was in her mid-sixties, just a few years younger than her husband chronologically, but spiritually she was decades his junior. She exuded vigor. Her skin possessed a cinnamon stick burnish. The battle waged between freckles and wrinkles for domination of her face was about to be won by the chisels. The flesh around her mouth was as crumbly as a Roquefort cheese – she either smiled or smoked a lot. There persisted in her an undeniable seductiveness..

"What was your job before you became a gardener?"

"I was a Navy wife."

"Mrs. Drayton, did you type a letter to your son in mid-December during the period he was at OCS?"

"I did."

"Was there more than one letter in that time period that you typed to him?"

"Definitely not. In December I prepare our annual family newsletter with all the happenings of the preceding year. I was so busy with that I only sent James that one bit of mail before he came home for Christmas."

"Did that letter you wrote and typed contain anything more than family news?"

"Yes, it contained my case against the Department of Defense. James asked me for a list and I prepared one for him."

"Why did he request this list? I'm not asking you to speculate. Only answer the question if you know."

"I can answer it. James wanted it for a meeting with the Great Lovers, to shore up his case to them."

"How did you know about the Great Lovers?"

"James wrote to me about them and what they wanted to accomplish."

"Do you have those letters?"

"No. I always crumpled them up and put them in the compost. I didn't want the Admiral to read them."

"Didn't he see them in the mailbox?"

"We live at the end of a dirt road a quarter mile long. They hold our mail at the post office, and I pick it up."

"Why did you keep the letters from your husband?"

"The Admiral would not have approved of the Great Lovers."

"Why not?"

"He worships the tradition that warps...weakens...kills his service every day." Mrs. Drayton's lips tightened around the fighting words.

"How many children do you have, Mrs. Drayton?"

"I had four. Now I have three. James was the youngest."

"Mrs. Drayton, did your son always want to be in the Navy?"

"Yes."

"The FBI profile suggests he joined the Navy to sabotage his father. Do you agree with that?"

"Absolutely not. For years I had filled James's head with my ideas for the Navy, the ones my husband wouldn't listen to. These became the core beliefs of the Great Lovers. In a way, I joined the Navy when James did."

"Are you the brains behind the Great Lovers?"

"I'm no genius, but the ideals started with me. James made them his own. The society was his idea, as well as the name."

"Did he tell you how he selected the accused?"

"No. But he had great empathy. He must have detected sympathy, and perhaps pain, in them that made them susceptible to new ideas. I do know how he decided on choosing four people though."

"How?"

"My family has lived on Martha's Vineyard since the Eighteenth Century. The family business was whaling. When my father said grace at the table, he always concluded the way his father and grandfather did. After he thanked God, he thanked the Four Winds, saying our ships, our fortunes and our lives are at their mercy. When James selected Rayna, Tate, Jennifer and Julius, he said that he had found his Four Winds, who would spread our ideas throughout the Navy."

"If they were the Four Winds, then what was James?"

She looked puzzled, then found an answer that clearly pleased her.

"James was the ocean."

"Did you or James ever talk of resorting to violent means to institute change?"

"Never."

"Was James suicidal? Did he want to die young?"

"He often talked about dying young. I think he had a foreknowledge of his own early death. That's why he was determined to get as much as he could from life. Crucial to his enjoyment of life was helping others. Look at what he did for these young people and the others on his ship. He would never take his own life or anyone else's."

"Thank you, Mrs. Drayton. I have no further questions."

LCDR Brandt did not cross examine her. She had nothing to gain from interrogating this lady.

The Four Winds were extremely still.

Thomas announced that the defense rested. Ms. Brandt did not wish to present any rebuttal witnesses. All that remained were the closing arguments. First the defense, then the prosecution. Judge Eagleeye told Thomas to be ready to make his at 0900 the next morning.

*

0900 WEDNESDAY/ THOMAS'S CLOSING ARGUMENT

"President and members of the court-martial, as you attempt to determine the difference between free speech and mutiny, between standing up for what we believe and insubordination, I think it is useful to hear about an American hero. At a meeting of the Joint Chiefs, just after President Clinton's election, all of the Chiefs came out, as it were, against gay and lesbian integration. The Chiefs, including General Powell, spoke their minds, even though the President-elect had already declared his desire to open the service. General Powell said he was honor bound to give his views, even though they weren't what the President wanted to hear. I disagree with his views, but I respect his willingness to express what he believes.

"Ensigns Rayna Washington, Tate Gunderson, Julius Chavez, and Jennifer Levy have beliefs, like General Powell. Like him, they are honor bound to attempt to put their ideas in practice someday. Of course, they will follow orders from a superior officer. Yet, one day, if they remain in the military, if they live up to their early promise, the accused will be the Admirals issuing the orders. I, for one, hope they have some ideas, some beliefs, in their heads when they attain that rank. I also hope that the Great Lovers of the Navy will be honor bound to tell even the President their views and will honorably fight for them.

"I beseech you. Do not punish the accused for loving what is right in the Navy and for seeking to redress what is wrong for the sake of the overall mission. Don't blame them for having opinions. Find the accused not guilty."

*

1030 WEDNESDAY/ BRANDT'S CLOSING ARGUMENT

"James Drayton idolized Rupert Brooke, but he knew his hero was a bigot. He knew Rupert Brooke was a poet of the second or third rank. Even the words in his so-called war poems display zero acquaintance with the horror of actual warfare. Brooke's death in wartime, which lent his poetry some authority, was not even combat related.

"The four accused should have recognized these dangerous contradictions and the damaged mind that espoused them. Even if the accused were too lazy to investigate Rupert Brooke, they should have recognized the instability of James Drayton, a young man who put himself in the one position in the world that would make him most uncomfortable.

"Drayton and the accused thrived on secrets and conspiracy. The accused met with Drayton at meeting after meeting. Their society destroyed all its papers. This is contrary to our service's openness. These so-called Great Lovers wanted to end the Navy as we know it. And then one of them, the leader, died in an explosion that crippled the Navy in an important mission. This explosion's cause has never been adequately explained.

"You must find the defendants guilty of failure to report a mutiny, which they knew was taking place."

*

0800 THURSDAY/ THE VERDICT

The judge ordered us to stand and approach the president of the court-martial. We walked to a spot in front of the most senior of the members.

"Would the president of the court-martial announce the findings, please?" the judge asked.

The president read, "Of the specification and charge, this court-martial finds you not guilty. We recommend, however, that the accused be reprimanded sharply for their membership in a secret society, which we find to be disruptive to good order in the military, and for not reporting James Drayton's admission that he was gay. Although we find the beliefs of the Great Lovers Society to be mutinous in nature, no evidence was presented that the accused plotted the explosion on the *Determination* or that they took any real action to accomplish their mutinous ideas."

We collapsed into each other's arms. Thomas enfolded all four of us in his enormous embrace.

*

It is now sixteen years later, and we are all still in the Navy. We have loved the Navy's saltiest and most venerable traditions; and we have loved making the Navy change. Our commendations for actions in wartime have long ago undone the taint of the reprimand given us in the court-martial.

On the day that Don't Ask, Don't Tell was finally repealed a few months ago, each of us approached our commands to volunteer to recruit gay, lesbian and bisexual service members. Our offer was gratefully accepted. We did it for James, and we did it for our country.

Mrs. Drayton had considered scattering James's ashes at Rupert Brooke's grave in Skyros. In the end, however, she asked the Four Winds to disperse them to all the oceans of the world.

April 2012

ABOUT THE AUTHOR

David Norton Stone is a graduate of Yale University, Navy Officer Candidate School in Newport, Rhode Island and the University of Connecticut School of Law. He lives in New York City and Warwick, Rhode Island.